S0-AFR-732

A MOMENT OF MADNESS—AND MAGIC

It was as if Susan were drowning in sensation. The thought flashed across her mind: "I must be crazy. I don't even *know* this man."

His skin was coppery in the glow of the fire, his eyes dark with mystery and promise. In that enchanted moment he seemed to her almost a god, a strange and mythical being, enormous and overwhelming, before whose power she bent as a reed before the wind. But the feel of his body was very real against hers, as was the growing, throbbing ache his touch was arousing deep inside her. She held him close, all the length of her slim body pressed against her. Her mouth sought his again and again.

And Susan knew that whoever this stranger was, whatever he wanted to do, she wanted him . . .

JOAN WOLF is a native of New York City who presently resides in Milford, Connecticut, with her husband and two children. She taught high school English in New York for nine years and took up writing when she retired to rear a family. She is the author of two other Rapture Romances, SUMMER STORM and CHANGE OF HEART.

Dear Reader:

It's a new Rapture! Starting this month we'll be bringing you only the best four books each month, by well-known favorite authors and exciting new writers, and to demonstrate our commitment to quality we've created a new look for Rapture: bigger, bolder, brighter. But don't judge our books by their covers—open them up and read them. We've used the comments and opinions we've heard from *you*, the reader, to make our selections, and we know you'll be delighted.

Keep writing to us. Your letters have already helped us bring you better books—the kind you want—and we depend on them. Of course, we are always happy to forward mail to our authors—writers need to hear from their fans!

And don't miss any of the inside story on Rapture. To tell you about upcoming books, introduce you to the authors, and give you a behind-the-scenes look at romance publishing, we've started a *free* newsletter, *The Rapture Reader*. Just write to the address below, and we will be happy to send you each issue.

Happy reading!

The Editors
Rapture Romance
New American Library
1633 Broadway
New York, NY 10019

BELOVED STRANGER

by

Joan Wolf

RAPTURE ROMANCE

NEW AMERICAN LIBRARY

PUBLISHER'S NOTE

This novel is a work of fiction. Names, characters, places, and incidents either are the product of the author's imagination or are used fictitiously, and any resemblance to actual persons, living or dead, events, or locales is entirely coincidental.

NAL BOOKS ARE AVAILABLE AT QUANTITY DISCOUNTS
WHEN USED TO PROMOTE PRODUCTS OR SERVICES.
FOR INFORMATION PLEASE WRITE TO PREMIUM MARKETING DIVISION.
NEW AMERICAN LIBRARY. 1633 BROADWAY.
NEW YORK. NEW YORK 10019.

Copyright © 1984 by Joan Wolf

All rights reserved

SIGNET, SIGNET CLASSIC, MENTOR, PLUME, MERIDIAN
AND NAL BOOKS are published by New American Library,
1633 Broadway, New York, New York 10019

First Printing, March, 1984

1 2 3 4 5 6 7 8 9

PRINTED IN THE UNITED STATES OF AMERICA

Chapter One

The snow was coming down harder and harder and Susan Morgan was beginning to worry. She had left the White Mountains ski lodge of a school friend a few hours earlier, when the snow had been light and flaky. Now, however, it was beginning to look like a blizzard, and she was afraid she had been foolish to insist upon leaving. She had been traveling the side roads; she decided she had better try to get over to 91 instead.

Half an hour later she knew she wouldn't make it. She couldn't see a foot in front of her and there had been no other cars on the road. "I'm the only one idiotic enough to come out in a blizzard," she muttered as she hunched over the wheel of her old Volkswagen and tried to keep on the road. Two minutes later she slid into a ditch and the car stalled. She could not get it started again.

Susan could feel her stomach clench with fear. She tried the car one more time and got no response. "Well," she said aloud, trying to be calm, "the choice is to sit here and freeze to death or to try and find help." She did not want to get out of her car but chill was already beginning to set in and she knew she couldn't stay. She leaned over to her suitcase in the backseat and fished out ski mittens, goggles, hat and scarf. She bundled herself up as warmly as she could and then resolutely stepped out into the raging storm.

She walked for twenty minutes without seeing a house, a car or a gas station. She had never been so cold in her entire twenty-one years. The only thing that kept her going was the thought of her mother. *I can't die,* she kept repeating fiercely to herself. *I can't do that to Mother. Not after Sara.*

When she was absolutely certain that she couldn't walk another step, she saw the lights of a house at the top of the hill on her left. It took the last remnant of willpower to get her to the door. She leaned against it for a moment, summoning the strength to knock. When the door opened she almost fell into the room.

"Dios!" said a startled male voice.

Susan tried to say something but her face felt frozen. Her teeth were chattering like castanets. "All right," the deep voice said practically, "first let's get you out of those wet clothes."

Susan's fingers didn't seem to be moving and so the stranger efficiently stripped her of hat, scarf, gloves, coat and one sweater. Her wool slacks below her jacket were caked with snow. He said, "Wait here," disappeared for a minute and came back with a large terrycloth bathrobe and a pair of wool socks. "Come over to the fire and let me check you for frostbite," he said, and she followed on trembling legs.

"Can you get those slacks off?" he asked.

"I—I think so." Her face and fingers were beginning to tingle and she managed to unzip her wet plaid slacks.

The stranger handed her the bathrobe. "Put that on and sit down," he said matter-of-factly.

She did as he asked and he knelt to pull off her socks and inspect her toes. His hands felt very warm against her icy feet. He put the wool socks on her and looked up. "Let me see your hands." She held her hands out and he took them in his own large warm ones and carefully inspected first one side and then the other.

"Another five minutes and you'd have been in trouble," he said. "Sit right there and I'll get you a glass of brandy."

Susan huddled inside the warm robe, flexed her feet inside the warm socks, and slowly the feeling returned to her body. The brandy burned going down but she finished it all and then looked over at her rescuer and attempted a smile. "I don't know how to thank you. I thought it was all over for me."

"It almost was," he said noncommittally, and reached over to feel her hands. "I'll run you a bath. That should finish thawing you out. And then you can tell me what the devil you were doing wandering around in a blizzard."

"I was being stupid," she said bitterly. He gave her an assessing look before he went inside. In a minute she heard the sound of running water.

The bath was hot and wonderful and she could feel all her muscles relaxing. She stayed until the water began to cool off and then she got out. The collar of her turtleneck cotton jersey was wet and cold and she couldn't stand the thought of putting it on again, so she put on only her bra and panties and wrapped the bathrobe firmly around her. It was enormous. She put the wool socks on her feet; they were enormous too. She looked in the medicine cabinet and found a comb with which she smoothed out her shoulder-length hair. Then she opened the bathroom door and went, with a little uneasiness, toward the living room. All she had noticed about her host before was that he was very tall and dark and that he had a deep, mellow speaking voice that seemed to hold the very faintest trace of an accent. She stepped into the living room. "That felt marvelous," she said to the man who was sitting comfortably in front of the fire.

He turned at the sound of her voice and looked at her out of eyes that were very large and very brown. He saw a small girl, whose slenderness was almost comically swathed in the folds of his terry-cloth bathrobe. Her delicate face was framed by curtains of straight, pale brown hair. He grinned. "You look lost in that robe," he said.

Susan smiled back. He had the darkest eyes she had ever seen, and the most beguiling smile. His teeth were very white against his warm olive skin. "I know," she replied. "But all my things were wet."

"We'll hang them in front of the fire to dry tonight," he said, and gestured. "Come over and sit down."

He was sitting on one end of the worn, comfortable-looking sofa and she walked slowly across the room and seated herself on the other end. She tucked her legs under her, sedately arranged her robe and turned to look at him.

"Let me put another log on the fire," he said, "and then you can tell me your story." He stood up and went to get wood from the basket. Susan watched him silently. He was a spendid-looking man, in his middle to late twenties, tall and dark-haired, with glowing golden skin. The hips that were encased in a worn pair of jeans were slim but the shoulders under the plaid flannel shirt looked enormous.

He dropped the wood on the fire, poked it a few times and then came back to the sofa. He sat down where he had been before, turned to her and said, "Well?"

She sighed. "My name is Susan Morgan," she began dutifully, "and I was staying with a college friend at her family's ski lodge up in Franconia Notch. When I left this morning it was only snowing lightly. I had no idea it was going to get this bad."

"You should have gotten off the road hours ago."

"I know." She looked embarrassed. "I was—kind of preoccupied and I didn't really notice how heavy the snow was becoming."

A look of faint amusement settled over his face. "Women," he said. "They shouldn't be allowed behind the wheel of a car."

Susan sat up a little straighter. "I was—thinking of something else," she said defensively.

The amusement on his face deepened. "You must have been if you didn't even notice a blizzard."

Susan bit her lip. "Please don't try to make me feel stupider than I do already. I can't thank you enough for rescuing me."

He shrugged. He had the widest shoulders she had ever seen. *"De nada,"* he said. "I am glad I was here."

"Is this your lodge?" she asked curiously.

"No. I'm only renting it for a week." He smiled at her, that unbelievable smile, and said softly, "My name is Ricardo."

"Hello, Ricardo," Susan said, and smiled back. It was impossible not to smile when he did, she thought. "You're here all alone?" she asked.

"Yes."

She looked at him gravely and the large, incredible brown eyes looked back. Susan nodded her head. "It's nice to be alone sometimes," she said softly. "That's why I like cross-country skiing better than downhill."

He looked interested. "I have never done cross-country."

She smiled dreamily, her widely spaced gray eyes shimmering in the firelight. "It's lovely. So quiet. Only the trees and the sound of the skis. All the rest is just beautiful white silence."

"It does sound nice." He looked suddenly a little rueful. "Sometimes it's very hard to be alone, I find. I'll have to try cross-country."

"I'm sorry I barged in on you," she said a little awkwardly.

"You I do not mind." There was a note in his voice that made her breath catch suddenly. "Susan," he said experimentally, trying her name as if it were a foreign word. "Are you warm now?" He reached over to feel her hand. His own was lean and brown and very hard.

Susan had never been this physically conscious of a man in her entire life. The touch of his hand had been like an electrical charge. She cleared her throat. "I'm fine," she said. Then, feeling it necessary to say something, "Do you do a lot of skiing?"

He had removed his hand but he was now sitting halfway across the sofa. "When I get a chance, which is not often." He grinned at her. "I have a boss who is paranoid about my getting hurt. And I do like downhill. I like the speed of it."

A strand of straight dark hair had fallen over his forehead. She had a sudden urge to reach out and smooth it back. She retreated a little farther into her corner and searched for something else to say. Good manners forbade her asking him what his job was.

"Would you like something to drink?" he asked.

"If you're having something."

He got up from the sofa with the liquid grace of a dancer—or an athlete. She stared for a moment at the narrow outline of his hips in the low-slung jeans and then raised her face to his. "Some wine?" he asked softly.

"Okay." Their eyes met and for the first time there was tension between them. He turned to go to the kitchen and Susan looked into the blazing fire. He returned with two glasses of red wine and handed her one. He sat down next to her and stretched out his legs.

"I think the snow is stopping," he murmured as he sipped his wine.

"Is it? Good. I'm anxious to get to my mother's. I only have a few more days before I'm due back at college."

"Mmm?" he said deeply. His long lean body seemed perfectly relaxed. He was only inches away from her.

I should get up, Susan thought. She knew what was coming next. I should make it perfectly clear that I have no intention of falling into bed with him. But the fire was so drugging in its warmth; it made her feel so safe, so secure. She sipped her wine slowly and stared at the flames. When she finally turned, it was to find him watching her. He said nothing; neither did his eyes drop. They were filled with the light of the fire.

She gazed back, her small head tilted back, exposing her slender neck, her fine, shimmering hair spilling all around her shoulders. He slid his fingers into that hair. "It's like a child's," he murmured softly. "So soft. So very fine."

She drew back from him a little and he smiled at her, a lovely smile that quite turned her heart over. "Susan," he said, "*querida*. You needn't be afraid of me." She was getting lost in his eyes. His hand moved down to caress her throat and she closed her own eyes. The smoky smell of the fire filled her nostrils.

The brandy and the wine ran warm in her veins. She had never felt this way before in her life. His hand slid down between the robe and touched her breast. Susan's eyes flew open and he bent his head to kiss her.

It was as if she were drowning in sensation. The thought flashed across her mind: I must be crazy. I don't even *know* this man. But his mouth on hers was warm and gentle, his body against hers was broad and strong. All sense of strangeness left her. His eyes were brilliant in the firelight. His arms around her felt very secure. He is so big, she thought, so warm. The touch of his fingers on her breast was exquisite. He kissed her again and she relaxed against him, her arms sliding around his chest with a naturalness that would have amazed her if she had been capable of rational thought. The flannel of his shirt was soft under her palms, but she could feel the hardness of muscle through the fabric. His mouth was hard now as well, demanding, urgent. Susan's lips parted sweetly for him and one hand went up to caress the strong column of his neck.

The only light in the room was the glow given off by the fire, and when he laid Susan back against the cushions of the sofa and began to unbutton his shirt, she looked at him out of eyes that were wide and wondering. His skin was coppery in the glow of the firelight, his eyes dark with mystery and with promise. In that enchanted moment he seemed to her almost as a god, a strange and mythical being, enormous and overwhelming, before whose power she bent as a reed before the wind. But the feel of his warm brown body was very real against hers as was the growing, throbbing ache his touch was arousing deep inside her. The warm air from the fire was hot on her bare skin, the fabric of the sofa rough under her back. She held him close, all the length of her slim body pressed against him. Her mouth sought his again and a small whimper formed deep in her throat.

He heard the sound and pressed her back into the cushions of the sofa. Susan obeyed him blindly, seeking desperately for a release from the unbearably sweet ache he had wrought inside her.

"Dios!" The muffled exclamation from him came at the same time she felt a sharp shooting pain tear through her body. Her eyes flew open in shock and she tried to pull away, but he held her firmly. "It'll be all right," he muttered. "Hold on." And then, mixed with the pain, came a flooding wave of pleasure that made her body shake and her fingers press deeply into his back. "Oh," she whispered. "Oh."

There was silence in the room, then a log cracked and fell on the fire and he raised his head to look down at her. "You were a virgin," he said in an odd voice.

She felt sleepy and warm and peaceful. "Mmm," she answered dreamily.

"But why?"

She didn't pretend to misunderstand him. She smiled up into his puzzled face. "I don't know," she said simply.

He had been watching her steadily, seriously, but now he smiled as well, a slow smile that was as intimate as his touch had been. "It was magic," he said softly.

So he had felt that too. "Yes." Her eyes were very heavy.

He picked her up as if she weighed scarcely anything. "You are falling asleep," he said. "Come." And he carried her into the bedroom, wrapped her once again in his bathrobe and tucked her under the covers. "Good night, *querida*," he said. "Sleep well."

She awoke to the bright sun streaming in her bedroom window. It was ten-thirty according to her watch and with an exclamation of alarm she jumped out of bed. The snow had stopped and the world outside the window looked like a fairy tale. She walked into the living room rather tentatively, but Ricardo was gone. He had left her a note on the kitchen table. "The roads are plowed and I've gone to try to locate your car. Make yourself some breakfast." There was no signature. She walked back into the living room. Her clothes were spread on several chairs in front of the fire. When she felt them, they were dry. She looked at the blanket and pillow on the couch and knew where he had spent the night.

She dressed and went back to the kitchen, made herself a cup of instant coffee and sat down at the table. She should be horrified with herself, she thought. She had just slept with a man she didn't know, a man who was obviously anxious to see her on her way as quickly as he could. And yet she wasn't sorry. It had been—as he had said himself—magic.

It wasn't magic two hours later, however, when Ricardo returned. He brought a gust of cold air in the door with him and the grin he gave her was good-natured and slightly cocky. He stood by the door and stripped his gloves off. "We've got your car going," he said.

"Oh good." She walked slowly into the living room from the kitchen, trying to conceal her uneasiness. "How did you know where to look for it?"

"Simple," he replied. He came across the room, tracking snow all over the floor. "You said you were coming from the Notch and I knew you couldn't have walked far. Not in that storm." He unzipped his jacket. "It's down at the garage in town. I'll take you there after lunch."

"Fine," she replied quietly, "but I'm afraid there's nothing to eat. You only have coffee and bread and butter."

He fished in the capacious pocket of his jacket and brought out a small brown bag. "Ham and cheese." He handed it to her. "You can make some sandwiches."

She accepted the package. "All right." He followed her into the kitchen, talking cheerfully about her car. She made the sandwiches, listening to him with half an ear and trying to deal with her own sense of shock. It was hard to believe that the tender lover of last night was the same person as this tall and obviously tough young man who was lounging carelessly at his ease, waiting for her to serve him. She put a sandwich in front of him. "I'm afraid there isn't any mustard," she said expressionlessly.

"I eat out," he said, and bit into his bread with strong white teeth. "Where do you go to school?" he asked after half the sandwich was gone.

"Melford," she answered, naming a very old and very prestigious women's college.

"I see." He looked amused. "And are you studying political science so you can change the world?"

She looked at him levelly. "No. I'm studying English literature."

"Ah." He started on the other half of his sandwich.

"What do *you* do?" she asked to turn the tables.

He regarded her reflectively as he chewed. Then he said easily, "I play baseball. For the New York Yankees."

Her eyes widened and she put her coffee cup down. He had said his name was Ricardo. "You—you can't be Rick Montoya?" she said breathlessly.

"I can be and I am," he replied. He grinned at her engagingly. "You don't follow baseball, I take it."

"I knew your name."

He drained his coffee cup. "But not my face." He got up, went over to the refrigerator and took a piece of paper from the top of it. "These are my addresses," he said. "I'll be in Florida for spring training until April." He pointed to the Fort Lauderdale address. "The rest of the year I live in Stamford, Connecticut." He looked at her soberly. "Let me know if you need any help."

She stared at him blankly for a moment and then brilliant color stained her cheeks. Her eyes fell. She couldn't think of a thing to say.

"Come on," he said, "and we'll go get your car."

"Yes," she answered, and jumped to her feet. "Just a minute and I'll get my coat." Two minutes later she walked out the door with him and it slammed behind her, slammed forever on her night of magic.

Chapter Two

Susan reached her mother's house in Fairfield, Connecticut, by early that evening. Mrs. Morgan was surprised to see her. "You shouldn't have traveled in all this snow, dear," she said after Susan had kissed her at the door. "If I had known you were on the road, I would have been extremely worried."

"The highway was plowed all the way down," Susan said with a smile. "It wasn't bad at all. But I *could* use something to eat."

"Of course. Come into the kitchen." Susan followed her mother and watched as she efficiently prepared a cheese omelet for her daughter. "Did you enjoy your skiing?" Mrs. Morgan asked as she sat down across from Susan at the kitchen table.

"Yes. The Fosters are very nice people. I felt a little guilty about leaving you, though."

Her mother made a gesture of dismissal. "You musn't worry about me, dear. I've been very busy. The Talbotts had a dinner the other evening and then there was a meeting of the university women I had to attend."

Susan ate and listened to her mother chatter on. Apparently she had resumed her old busy schedule of meetings and lunches and teas and dinners. She was indomitable, Susan thought. The uncharacteristic

lethargy of Christmas week that had so worried her
daughter had quite disappeared.

"Are you teaching a full load this semester?" Susan
asked.

"Yes." When working, Mrs. Morgan was Dr. Helen
Morgan, Professor of Anthropology at the University
of Bridgeport. Susan's father had also been a professor at the university before his death a few years ago.

They moved into the living room and Susan curled
up on the sofa. "I was so pleased to hear of your
acceptance into the Honor Society, Susan," her
mother said warmly. "I'm proud of you. You worked
hard for it."

"I know." Susan made a face. "I may be just a member and you and Sara were presidents, but I'm pleased
with myself. It took me so *long* to finally get the
grades."

"I don't see why," her mother said briskly. "You're a
bright enough child."

Susan sighed. "I have such a hard time *finishing* a
test, Mother. I'm always still there when the time has
run out and usually I'm only half done. I think too
much and write too little."

Mrs. Morgan smiled abstractedly, her mind obviously elsewhere. "I've gone through Sara's clothes,"
she said after a minute, "and there are a number of
things that should fit you. The dresses will all be too
big, but the sweaters should be all right. And the suits
could be altered. And her new black coat. I've packed
a bag for you to take back to school with you."

"Oh Mother," Susan said weakly, "how can I wear
Sara's clothes?"

"She would want you to. I want you to." A shadow
crossed Mrs. Morgan's face. "I don't want to just give
them to the Salvation Army, Susan."

Susan had a brief vision of her sister's beautiful, vital face. She had loved clothes, loved shopping. "Of course you can't give her things to the Salvation Army," she said quickly. "I hadn't thought. I'll take them. They'll remind me of Sara."

For a brief moment it seemed as if Mrs. Morgan's eyes went out of focus and Susan knew it was not she that her mother was seeing. "It doesn't seem possible that she's gone," the older woman said at last in a low voice.

"I know." Susan sat still, helplessly watching her mother. There was nothing she could say, nothing she could do to comfort her. Sara was gone, killed instantly by an out-of-control trailer truck on the New England Thruway, and no one could fill her place.

Mrs. Morgan forced a smile. "You must be tired, dear, after that drive. Don't let me keep you up."

"I am rather tired." Susan rose slowly and went to kiss her mother's smooth cheek. "Good night, Mother."

"Good night, dear. Sleep well."

"I'll try," murmured Susan; the memory of how she had slept last night flashed into her mind. She wrenched her thoughts back into the present and slowly, resolutely, climbed the stairs to her bedroom.

Susan looked out the window of her dorm and sighed. It had been raining for five days and the new leaves on the trees looked heavy and green and limp. The weather was a perfect reflection of her mood. She stared blankly for a few more minutes at the paper she was trying to write for a poetry course and then reached into the desk drawer and drew out, once again, the lab report. There it was, clear and inescapable, the unwelcome news: she was pregnant.

Her first reaction had been anger. How could she
have been so *stupid*? Her second reaction had been
self-pity. Why me? I only did it once. From self-pity
she had progressed to her present state of mind,
which could be summed up by one question: what am
I going to do?

Ricardo had foreseen this possibility. He had told
her to get in touch with him, and given her his
address. The regular baseball season had opened a
few weeks ago. Susan, who had never followed baseball in her life, had taken to reading all she could get
her hands on about the New York Yankees and about
Ricardo Montoya in particular. Consequently, she
knew that he had signed a multimillion dollar contract
in February and that he had had a sensational spring.
The Yankees were universally expected to win the
American League Pennant this year.

Ricardo would be home in Stamford. Should she
write him?

She took out a fresh sheet of looseleaf notebook
paper and began to compose a letter. After three sen-
tences she stopped, looked at what she had written
and tore it up. "I sound like an idiot," she muttered
disgustedly. She stood up. "I *am* an idiot." She got her
raincoat from the closet and ran down the stairs. She
needed to get away from her own company.

The student lounge was more filled than usual due
to the rainy weather. Susan spotted a group of friends
and went over to join them. One girl had a copy of a
national news magazine on her lap and Susan felt a
jolt of shock when she looked down and saw the picture on the cover.

"May I see that for a moment, Lisa?" she asked
rather breathlessly.

"Sure," the other girl answered. "You can join in

the general drooling if you like. We've all just decided that *that* is the man we would most want to be stranded on a desert island with."

"Would you?" asked Susan, and stared down at the picture. Ricardo was wearing his baseball uniform but not the hat. His thick, straight, dark brown hair had fallen slightly forward over his forehead. He looked lean and brown and his smile was the irresistible grin that she remembered so vividly. But it was the eyes that caught and held you, the large, beautiful, thick-lashed brown eyes.

"You could travel halfway round the world and you wouldn't find another man like that," one of the girls was saying.

Susan cleared her throat. "Where is he from? I mean, he's not American, is he?"

"He's Colombian. Or his parents are Colombian. He was born in the States, so that makes him an American citizen. It's all in the article."

"May I borrow the magazine, Lisa? I'll give it back to you."

Lisa grinned. "Susie! Now we know why you find all your dates so uninteresting. You're holding out for Rick Montoya."

Susan could feel herself flushing and the other girl reached over to give her hand a quick squeeze. "Of course you can borrow it. But I do want it back."

"Lisa wants to hang Rick's picture over her bed," one of the other girls teased, and everyone laughed. About ten minutes later Susan made her escape, clutching the magazine securely under her arm. Up in the solitary shelter of her bedroom she read the cover story through. Then she went to lie on her bed and stare out at the rain. Rick Montoya. It was impossible to make herself believe that the man she had just read

about was the same man who had given her shelter
from the storm and had made such tender and rap-
turous love to her.

She couldn't write to him. Everything the article
said had removed him further and further from her.
He was wealthy from baseball, she knew that, but
according to the article, he had been born wealthy.
His father was a director of Avianca Airlines and he
had grown up partly in Bogotá and partly in New
York. He had been drafted by the Yankees after
college and had consistently been one of the best hit-
ters in baseball ever since. He averaged thirty-eight
home runs a season and had a lifetime batting average
of .320. Susan didn't know much about baseball but
she gathered from the article that these were highly
impressive statistics. He was twenty-eight years old.
He was unmarried, but according to this article, he
never lacked for feminine companionship. The
names of two or three of the world's most beautiful
models were listed as his frequent companions. No,
she couldn't write to him. She felt sure that all he
would do—all he *could* do, really—would be to offer
her money for an abortion.

Susan closed her eyes and blotted out the view of
the rain. An abortion. The temptation was so great. It
would solve all her problems. No one would ever have
to know. It was so easy, she thought, to be opposed to
abortion in general. It was so hard when the particular case was you. She thought of her mother. How
could she hit her with this? And after Sara. It wouldn't
be fair. It was, in fact, unthinkable. Morgans just did
not have babies out of wedlock. Period.

But she knew, too, deep in her soul, that she would
not have an abortion. It would solve all problems

except one. She would have to live with the knowledge of what she had done.

She remembered then having seen an advertisement in the *Bridgeport Post* for an organization called Birthright. It was a group set up to help girls like herself. Susan got up off her bed and washed her face. She would get the number from information and call Birthright, she thought. She'd make an appointment and go home this weekend. It was time to stop bemoaning her fate and do something about it.

Susan relaxed gratefully in the cool air conditioning of the small restaurant and sipped her iced tea. Outside the downtown Hartford street shimmered in the heat of August, but inside it was pleasantly cool and uncrowded. It was two-thirty in the afternoon, well past the regular lunch hour. Once she had finished her drink she could go home.

Home. Well, it *was* home, she thought, for two more months at least. She could only feel gratitude toward the middle-aged single woman who had provided a shelter home for her for the duration of her pregnancy. The people at Birthright had found her the home and a part-time job that enabled her to give Elaine something toward her board and room.

The baby inside her gave a kick and she shifted a little on her chair. She glanced up as the door opened and then froze in her seat. There was no mistaking that tall, lean figure, that shock of very dark brown hair. Almost instantly she bent her head and gazed furiously at the table, trying to hide her face. Consequently she didn't see the man notice her, frown and then start a leisurely but purposeful approach toward her table.

"Susan?" said a low, deep, mellow voice that was unnervingly familiar. And she had to raise her head.

"Yes," she said. "Ricardo. What a surprise to find you here." She was surprised to hear how composed she sounded.

"I had to see someone in the immigration office about a friend of mine." He gestured. "May I sit down?"

"I suppose so." She made her voice distinctly unenthusiastic but he didn't appear to notice. He pulled the chair out opposite her and sat. She stared resolutely at the saltshaker. She didn't have to look to know that those shrewd brown eyes were assessing the bulkiness of her stomach. If it had been winter, if she were wearing a coat, then she thought she might have hidden it. But in a light cotton dress she didn't have a chance.

He reached out and caught her left hand as it moved restlessly on the table. They both stared for a long minute at the slender, delicate hand, so conspicuously bare of rings. He raised his eyes to her face. "Is it mine?" he asked tensely.

She bit her lip. "Yes."

"*Dios!* I told you to let me know if this happened. I knew there was a chance of it."

His hand was still grasping hers and she tried to draw away. He didn't let go and she stared once again at the strong tan fingers that were gripping her wrist so efficiently, remembering the last time they had touched her. "There was really nothing you could do for me, Ricardo," she said, she hoped calmly. "I'm managing quite well on my own, thank you. There is no need to concern yourself about me."

He smiled at her words and it was not a smile of

good humor. "How are you managing, *querida?*" he asked.

She pulled her hand again and this time he let it go. She flattened her back and said evenly, "I went to an organization called Birthright. I didn't want to tell my mother what had happened. She would have been terribly upset." She put her hand up, from long habit, to push back her hair but it was already neatly tied at the nape of her neck. She let her hand fall again. "My older sister Sara was killed last year in a car accident," she explained flatly, "and Daddy died of a heart attack three years ago. So, you see, I'm the only one Mother has left. I've never been as bright as Sara, or as pretty and vivacious, but still I'm all Mother has left now. I just couldn't come home pregnant."

"Your mother would have been angry?" he asked noncommittally.

"No. Not angry. She would have been marvelous. But, underneath, she would have been so disappointed."

"You would be a failure in her eyes."

Startled, she looked up at him. Those remarkable brown eyes had a very understanding look to them. She put her elbows on the table and rested her chin on her hands. "I suppose so," she said ruefully. "I suppose it wasn't just Mother's feelings I was sparing."

"So you went to this Birthright," he said. "Why did you not get an abortion?"

"I just couldn't."

He nodded. "And so?"

"And so the people at Birthright were absolutely marvelous. I couldn't stay around home, for obvious reasons. They found me a shelter home here in Hartford. I came here after graduation." She smiled a little painfully. "I made it through graduation all right. I didn't start to really show that much until the fifth month. After graduation I told Mother I had an opportunity to go to Europe with a family as a combination nurse-tutor for two children. That's where she thinks I am. A friend of mine, who *is* in Europe, is periodically mailing postcards I wrote in advance. So there it is."

"Not quite." He looked at her levelly. The lines of his cheek and jaw looked suddenly very hard. "What are you planning to do with the baby?"

This was the hard part. A look of strain crept across her face, tightening the skin, making her nose look more prominent. She was very pale. "I'm going to give him up for adoption," she said in a very low voice.

There was a long silence during which she refused to look at him. Then, "Why?" he asked in a clipped kind of voice.

"Because it will be the best thing for the baby. It may not be the best thing for me, but it's not my interest I've got to look out for in this." Now she did look at him. "My best friend in high school was adopted. Her parents were two of the greatest people I've ever known. It is not possible to love a child more than they loved her—and her two adopted brothers as well. A child needs a stable loving family. He needs a mother and a father—not a full-time day-care center, which is all I could offer him. The agency I'm going through has a list as long as your arm of couples who are just *longing* for a baby." She compressed her lips. "I've thought about this long and hard, Ricardo, and it hasn't been an easy decision, but I know it's the right one. I'm going to give him up for adoption."

"You keep saying 'him.' Do you know it is a boy?"

"Yes, actually I do. I had an ultrasound and the way the picture came out you could tell."

He leaned across the table toward her and took her hand once more in his. "Susan." No one else, she thought, made her name sound as it did when Ricardo said it. "If you could keep the baby," he was going on, "would you?"

"Of course I would," she answered instantly. "I don't *want* to give him away, you know."

"Then marry me," he said.

Her eyes flew wide open in shock. She stared at his face. It looked perfectly serious. "What?" she said.

"You heard me. Marry me. Surely it is the obvious solution."

"To you, maybe, but not to me," she got out. "I hardly *know* you."

He laughed, a sound of genuine amusement. "You know me well enough," he said, and she felt herself flushing furiously.

"Don't be clever," she muttered. "You know what I mean."

"Listen, *querida*," he said patiently. He was very obviously the reasonable, intelligent male dealing with an unreasonable and very silly woman. "You said yourself that it is not your interest that concerns you. It is the welfare of the child. Well, I am the child's father. I am wealthy. I will take good care of him." He stared into her eyes and his own were suddenly commanding. "I do not want *my* son to be brought up by another man."

She felt the force of his will, of his personality, bearing down on her and, instinctively, she resisted. "I don't know," she said.

He sat back a little in his chair. "I could simply take the child and let my mother raise him," he said. "She would be delighted to have a grandchild to live with her. And, unlike your mother, she would not think I had disappointed her." His dark stare was unwavering, almost inimical. "Would you prefer that?"

She stared back, her own eyes clearly reflecting her confusion and her hurt. She couldn't answer him. Quite suddenly he smiled and his whole face was transformed. "Listen, *querida*," and now his voice was gentle, "I know this has been a very hard time for you. I am as much responsible as you and yet you have had to bear all the worry, all the pain. Let me take care of you now. I know you will be a good mother and, who knows, you may even come to like being a wife." His eyes sparkled. "I am not so bad, you know. Now what do you say? Do you want to keep this baby?"

Of course she wanted to keep her baby, more than anything else in the world. But what would the final price be? "Yes," she said. Her widely spaced gray eyes searched his worriedly. "What—what kind of marriage did you have in mind?"

He looked surprised. "Marriage is marriage," he said. "I didn't know there were different brands."

She could feel herself flushing. "I meant—did you expect it would be permanent?"

"Permanent?" he echoed. And then his eyes narrowed as comprehension struck him. "Do you mean would I expect to divorce you after the baby is born?"

"Well," said Susan. "Yes."

His mouth thinned. "No," he said flatly. "I would expect you to be my wife." He looked at her assessingly and she was terribly conscious of her bulky figure. "What are you afraid of?"

She closed her eyes for a minute. "Everything." Her voice was barely audible.

When she opened her eyes again his face had softened. "You are afraid to trust your future to me," he said very gently. "Don't worry, little one. I will take good care of you." He reached out and touched her cheek lightly. "We will have a son—the son we made together." He picked up her hand and kissed the inside of her wrist. "You did not find me so disagreeable once. It will be like that again."

The touch of his fingers, his mouth, brought back disturbing memories. "We really *don't* know each other. Do—do you still think we could make it work?" she asked uncertainly.

"Of course. Why ever should we not?"

Why ever? Susan thought blankly. And, really, what was her alternative? She looked up into his dark eyes. "Well—all right," she said.

He smiled at her and she felt the corners of her mouth lifting in response. "Good girl," he said. "We will do very well together. And now, why don't we go along to your shelter home and collect your things? You might as well come back to Stamford with me now." He signaled the waitress for her check.

Susan was a little nonplussed. She had been making her own decisions for so long now, it was a little bewildering to have someone move in so efficiently. It was also, she thought a little wryly as he paid her bill and pulled out her chair, rather pleasant. She wouldn't at all mind being bossed about for a while. She was very weary of managing on her own. Nevertheless, she said firmly, as they stepped out into the heat of the city street, "I have to go talk to the people in the agency first. They've been very good to me."

"Do you want to go now?"

"Yes."

"Very well," he said, and, putting a hand on her back, guided her toward a forest-green Mercedes. "I'll come with you. I don't want anyone trying to change your mind."

God, Susan thought, what were they going to think at the agency when she turned up with Rick Montoya? It really would be easier if he stayed in the car. She glanced sideways at the set of his mouth and decided not to argue. She didn't have the energy. "What is the address?" he asked, and she gave it to him.

Chapter Three

The following week was one of the most stressful and unsettling times in Susan's entire life. It started with the ride to Stamford in Ricardo's car. They had left Susan's old Volkswagen behind; Ricardo assured her easily that he would have someone pick it up.

"What are we going to tell people?" she asked him as she sat back against the comfortable beige upholstery of the Mercedes.

He flicked a glance at her before he went back to watching the road. "What do you mean?"

She felt horribly embarrassed. "I don't want people to know the truth," she said unhappily. "Couldn't we say we've known each other for a while?"

"Oh, I see." A faint smile touched his mouth. "I don't see why we couldn't say that, *querida*. We'll say we met in the autumn and quarreled in January. All the rest can be the truth—your keeping the news of your pregnancy secret and so forth."

"Yes, I suppose that would do." She felt her cheeks grow hot. "What are people going to *think* of me?"

He chuckled. "People will think very well of us. After all, we're doing the proper thing."

"They will think well of *you* for making an honest

woman of me. They won't think so well of me, I'm afraid."

He shrugged. "It is not important what other people think." He glanced at her again, his eyes warm and bright in the late sunshine. "*I* know what kind of woman you are, *querida*. That is all that matters."

Susan felt a sudden flash of gratitude. After all, he had never even questioned whether or not this baby was his. She wondered how many other men would have behaved so gracefully under the present circumstances. She sighed a little and he reached out to cover her small hand with his strong, warm one. "Don't worry," he said easily. "It will all work out."

They were married four days later in Stamford. Joe Hutchinson, the second baseman on Ricardo's team, and Maggie Ellis, Susan's closest friend, stood up for them. It was accomplished very quietly, with absolutely no press leaks, and the only other person present in the church was Mrs. Morgan.

Susan had been extremely apprehensive about breaking the news to her mother, but the reality had not proved as dreadful as her imagination had predicted. Mrs. Morgan was visibly shocked by the sight of her pregnant daughter, but Ricardo had taken charge, and almost before she realized what was happening, Susan found herself sitting on the porch while her mother served them lemonade.

"It was a foolish quarrel," Ricardo was saying gravely. "And it was very wrong of Susan not to have contacted me when she knew she was to have a child." He gave her a reproachful look and sipped his lemonade. "But now we are reconciled and all will be well." He looked serenely at Susan's mother out of large dark eyes. "May I have some more lemonade? It's very good."

"Of course." Mrs. Morgan moved to rise but Susan forestalled her.

"I'll get it, Mother," she said hastily, and disappeared in the direction of the kitchen. When she returned, after a rather longer time than was necessary, Ricardo and her mother were talking comfortably about South America. Both Susan's parents had been anthropologists and when she was a child they had periodically disappeared for stretches of a year at a time into the jungles of the Amazon.

"I have never been to the Brazilian jungle," Ricardo said as Susan settled down again into her chair. He had accepted his drink with a perfunctory smile. He's used to being waited on, she thought, as she sat back and prepared to listen.

The discussion was pleasant and civilized, and from the way her mother looked at him, Susan realized that Ricardo knew what he was talking about. When they left he gave Mrs. Morgan a smile that visibly moved her. Susan was beginning to suspect that he got a lot of mileage out of that beguiling grin.

"Mother liked Ricardo," she wrote in her journal that evening. She had been keeping it ever since she was sixteen, as a way of sifting through, assimilating and comprehending the raw material of her life. And life for Susan, daughter of two educated and brilliant super-achievers, had never been easy. She loved her parents dearly, she had admired and adored her elder sister Sara, but she was different from the rest of the family, slower, more introspective, more deeply feeling. The journal had become essential to the daily routine of her life.

She looked now at the sentence she had written and

then added, "and what is perhaps more surprising, she was impressed by him. There is an extraordinary quality about him that goes beyond his looks. He simply sat there on our porch, drinking lemonade and wearing perfectly ordinary-looking clothes, and one somehow had the impression that he was conferring an honor on us by his very presence." She frowned a little as she thought. "It's not that he's conceited," she wrote then. "He's not. But he has—perhaps presence is the best word for it. Whatever it is, it did a job on Mother. She's coming to the wedding and she never even objected when she learned her Protestant Yankee daughter was going to be married by a Catholic priest. I suppose the fact that said Protestant daughter is also seven months pregnant had a lot to do with her compliance."

Susan put down her pen and looked out the window of her bedroom. The stars were very bright in the moonless sky. Ricardo was playing a night game and wouldn't be home until after midnight. She thought now that it was odd she hadn't thought of staying with her mother until the wedding. Her mother hadn't suggested it either. They had both simply fallen in behind Ricardo like good soliders, nodding yes to whatever he suggested.

Extraordinary, she thought, and yawned. She was very tired. She looked one more time at her diary entry and then closed the book. She got into the wide bed in the big bedroom Richardo had given to her and tried to get comfortable. He hadn't even suggested that she share his room. The baby kicked, hard, and Susan smiled ruefully. In her present condition she was scarcely alluring, she thought. And then she fell asleep.

* * *

The wedding went very smoothly and afterward Ricardo took everyone out to lunch in a very expensive Greenwich restaurant. Then Joe Hutchinson, Maggie and Mrs. Morgan left and the new Mr. and Mrs. Montoya returned home. However, Ricardo only stopped long enough to drop Susan and change clothes. The Yankees were playing a twilight double header that evening at six. Ricardo had to be at the stadium by five. "Don't wait up for me," he told her pleasantly as he dropped a kiss on her cheek. "I'll be late."

"All right." She stood at the door as he walked toward the Mercedes he had left parked in the circular drive in front of the house. "Good luck!" she called, and he gave her a grin before he slid in behind the wheel.

Susan closed the door and slowly walked back to the living room. Maria, the Colombian maid who did the cooking and cleaning for Ricardo, had been given the afternoon off in honor of the wedding, and Susan was alone. She stood silently in the middle of the living room and stared at the lovely marble fireplace. This was "home." It didn't feel like home, was nothing at all like the comfortable old clapboard house she had grown up in, but she was going to have to grow accustomed to it, she told herself firmly. She looked carefully around the large, high-ceilinged room. It was lovely, she admitted. The molding and wainscoting were beautiful, as was the shining wood floor. It just was far more elegant than what she was accustomed to. Far more rich.

Ricardo's home was a stately Georgian colonial, built of brick and slate and set on a wooded couple of acres in north Stamford. He had bought it two years ago, he told her when she first arrived home with him, and his mother had furnished it for him. The furniture was not the style Susan would have chosen, but she found herself liking the carved Spanish pieces very much.

Perhaps it was a good sign: she would have something in common with the mother-in-law she had yet to meet. Ricardo's mother had lived in Bogotá since his father's death and came north only once or twice a year to visit her son. Ricardo also had two sisters, both quite a bit older than he, and both married and living in Bogotá. "When the season's over we'll go visit them," he had told her casually.

"Ricardo, the baby is due in October," she protested.

"We'll go for Christmas, then, and bring him along. My mother will be thrilled. You know how women are about babies."

It was not a visit that Susan looked forward to. Ricardo's mother might be thrilled to see the baby, but Susan very much doubted if she'd be thrilled to see the bride her son had so hastily wedded.

Oh well, she thought, as she walked slowly about the downstairs rooms of her new home, no use borrowing trouble. I'll cross that bridge when I come to it. She passed through the large dining room, which also boasted a marble fireplace, and into the two rooms she was most familiar with: the breakfast room, where they ate their meals, and the family room with its lovely french doors leading out to the slate patio. "It's scarcely what one would call a starter home," she said out loud with a laugh of real amusement.

There was only one room on the first floor that she hadn't been in and that was the study. She walked in now and looked around slowly. The room was paneled and lined with bookshelves. Susan went over to one wall and looked at the titles; they were almost exclusively nonfiction. There were a number of books, both in Spanish and English, about Latin American politics. There were quite a lot of books on sports; not just baseball but soccer, tennis, golf and skiing. There was an Encyclopedia Americana and a full set of Sherlock Holmes. There was a small assortment of best-selling thriller-type novels. My God, thought Susan. There is so much I don't know about him. She collapsed heavily into a comfortable leather armchair and stared at a photograph of Ricardo that was hanging on the wall. It looked as if it were a newspaper photo that had been blown up and framed. It showed what was clearly a moment of victory; the three men in the picture were all laughing and one of them was pouring a bottle of champagne over Ricardo's head. His face, dark, vibrant, filled with triumph, was the dominant point of the photograph. Susan looked at that thoroughly male picture and inwardly she quaked.

How on earth were they going to build a marriage, she thought almost despairingly. If she had searched the earth over, it would have been impossible for her to find a person so utterly opposite to her. She was quiet and introspective, reserved and shy. That night in the blizzard had been completely out of character for her.

She thought of that night now and wondered with deep bewilderment how she had ever come to behave as she had. Over the last months it had become only a hazy memory, a dizzy recollection of warmth and smoke and the deep timbre of a man's voice. Her body heavy now with child, her senses dulled by advanced pregnancy, she couldn't begin to understand what had possessed her.

It was because of that night, however, that she was
here, in the home of Ricardo Montoya, a man whose
way of thinking and looking and relating to things was
completely opposed to hers. It was frightening.

She left the library and went upstairs. There were
five bedrooms on the second floor, each with its own
bathroom. Susan had been using the one next to
Ricardo's and now she hesitated and went into the
empty room that belonged to her husband. She had
peeked into it swiftly during the tour of the house he
took her on when first she arrived, but now she
looked around more carefully.

It was a thoroughly masculine room, with large oak
furniture and colorful woven material on the bed and
at the windows. An oil painting hung on the wall
facing the bed, a picture of a house nestled among
high, green mountains and very blue sky.

There was a clutter of loose change and papers on
the dresser, and on the floor, in front of the closet, lay
the suit that Ricardo had just taken off. His socks and
shoes were on the floor in front of the big upholstered
chair. Susan, who was innately tidy, bent awkwardly to
pick up the clothes. They were all creased from lying
in a heap. He might have hung them up, she thought
irritably. Now they would have to be sent out to the
cleaners. She folded the clothes neatly and laid them
on the bed. There was a book on the night table and
she went to look at it. *Report on El Salvador*, she read.
She picked it up, read the cover and then replaced it
on the table. She looked one more time around the
large, sunny room and then went next door to her
own bedroom.

There was a large mirror hanging over the dresser
in this room and Susan walked over to look in it.

"Some bride," she said ironically as she regarded her own reflection.

She actually looked very nice. Her skin had tanned to a pale honey from sitting out in Elaine's small yard and her shimmering light brown hair framed a face that had filled out a little with imminent motherhood. She looked, Susan thought, disgustingly healthy. But not even the expensive pale pink suit her mother had bought her could disguise her advanced pregnancy.

Susan kicked off her shoes and sighed with relief to stand barefoot again. She felt so small in comparison to Ricardo that she had bought much higher heels than she was accustomed to wearing. She took off her suit and hung it carefully in the closet. Then, wearing only her slip, she went over to the bed and lay down. There was a lovely breeze coming in the open window and she suddenly felt very tired. In two minutes, Susan was asleep.

When she awoke it was dark and she was feeling hungry. She showered, put on a smocked sun dress and thongs and went downstairs to the kitchen. She made herself a sandwich and then went into the family room and switched on the television. She looked at her watch. It was almost nine o'clock. The second game of the doubleheader should still be on.

It was the first time Susan had ever watched Ricardo play. Baseball had not been a sport anyone in her family ever watched and she was entirely unfamiliar with the routine of major league ball. She knew the basic rules of the game, had learned them almost by osmosis as does every American child, but the names and the tactics and the teams and the rivalries—all of these had remained obscure. She had refrained scrupulously from watching Ricardo before now; it had been almost a superstition that she should not allow him to come even that close to her. But now she sat back, munched her sandwich and prepared to watch.

It took her awhile to sort out what was happening. It took her awhile as well to sort out the strange feeling she had whenever Ricardo appeared on the screen, swinging a bat, looking relaxed and confident and surprisingly graceful.

"Montoya's the key to the pennant," the announcer was saying. "As long as he stays healthy, the Yankees are practically unbeatable."

"It's his consistency that's so amazing," another voice put in. "Day in, day out, always the same. It's pulled the club together, that evenness, that reliability."

"Yep. George was saying the other day that he doesn't grudge Rick a penny of what he's paying him."

The pitcher was peering in at the plate now and then began his windup. The ball was released and Susan watched in horror as Ricardo flung himself to the ground. She pressed her hand to her stomach and held her breath as he climbed slowly to his feet. He signaled to the bench that he was all right and began to dust his clothes. The entire stadium was roaring its disapproval at the pitcher. Ricardo looked perfectly calm.

"Carter doesn't want Rick to crowd the plate," commented the announcer. "He's moved him back a step with that pitch."

The pitcher went into his windup once more. Ricardo swung, a smooth, almost elegant motion, and there was the sound of a sharp *crack*.

"That's it!" the announcer cried jubilantly. "That one's gone." Ricardo began to jog around the bases, seemingly oblivious to the uproar of hysteria that had filled the huge stadium. When he crossed home plate there was a lineup of teammates to meet him. He shook hands, grinning that now familiar irresistible grin, and then he tipped his hat at the crowd. He never once glanced at Ben Carter, who was standing on the mound looking extremely unhappy.

"That'll be the last time Carter tries to brush Montoya back," the announcer said with a chuckle.

"Rick *does* have a way about him," the other voice said. "And now here's Price. The score is two—nothing, Yankees."

Susan sat through the remainder of the game, becoming increasingly fascinated. It was such an orderly sport, she thought; there was something very satisfying about the precision of all its movements, the way each man functioned individually yet as part of the whole. She watched the way the infield shifted as one to accommodate the different players. She watched the way Joe Hutchinson stepped out of the way to allow Ricardo, the center fielder, to take a high fly ball unimpeded. She watched the swiftness and precision of the Yankee infield effortlessly executing a double play from third to second to first. It was, she thought, an immensely satisfying spectacle. She had always understood the satisfaction of playing a sport. Now for the first time she was beginning to appreciate the pleasures of watching.

After the game was over Susan went upstairs and wrote in her journal for over an hour. When she finally put down her pen she went over to the window and looked out. There was no sign of Ricardo. She began to feel sorry for herself. This was certainly not the wedding night every young girl dreams of. She was very lonely.

As she was leaning forward to pull down the shade the lights of a car lit up the drive. Ricardo was home. For some inexplicable reason, Susan began to feel apprehensive. She stayed sitting at the desk, immovable, until she heard the sound of his feet on the stairs. The footsteps stopped outside her door.

He must have seen that her light was on, for he called softly, "Susan? Are you still awake?"

"Yes," she called back. Her voice sounded strange and she cleared her throat.

Her door opened and he stood on the threshold. She noticed a little nervously how wide his shoulders were. "Will you make me a sandwich?" he asked. "I'm starving."

Quite suddenly she relaxed. "Of course I will," she said, and smiled at him. "Haven't you eaten since lunch?" she asked as they walked down the stairs.

"No. I don't like to play on a full stomach." He seated himself comfortably at the kitchen table and watched her cut up some cold chicken.

"I watched the game," she said as she put the sandwich in front of him. "What would you like to drink?"

"Milk, please." He took a bite and chewed. "I didn't think you watched baseball."

"I haven't—until now." She put two glasses of milk on the table and sat down herself. "Why did that pitcher throw that ball at you? The announcer seemed to think it was deliberate."

"It was." He swallowed some milk, looked at her expression and chuckled. "Don't look so horrified, *querida*. Baseball is a constant war between the pitcher and the batter and one of the battles is over who has control of the plate. The batter likes to get close because it makes life more difficult for the pitcher. When the batter gets too close, however, the pitcher has to try to move him back."

"By throwing the ball at him?"

"Well, that is one way."

Susan drank some milk. "That was when you hit a home run," she said.

He raised a black eyebrow. "I do not like having a ninety mile per hour fastball thrown at my head."

"I should think not," she replied fervently.

They sat for a few more minutes in silence as Ricardo finished his sandwich. Then Susan said, "Did you ever think that this was how you'd be spending your wedding night?"

He laughed, his teeth very white in his tanned face. "No. But I'm not complaining." He finished his milk. "Are there any cookies?"

She got out some cookies for him and refilled his glass. He looked up and caught her gaze. "We are not exactly a romantic duo, are we?" he asked humorously.

Susan's face suddenly lit with laughter. "No, we're not." She laid her hand on the pronounced curve of her stomach.

His eyes followed her hand. "You are carrying my child. You've fed me and listened to me." His dark eyes held twin devils in their depths. "The rest can wait," he said.

Susan felt her breath catch in her throat and her body tensed. Then he leaned back in his chair and stretched. "Come," he said. "It's late and I've kept you up too long." She started to tidy up and he made an impatient gesture. "Leave it. Maria will clean up in the morning." He held the kitchen door for her. "Your job, *querida*," he said as they went up the stairs, "is to take good care of my son."

Chapter Four

Susan's baby was born on the day the Yankees won the American League Pennant. Ricardo took her to the hospital at five in the afternoon and then left for the stadium. She didn't see him again until five in the morning, after the baby had been born.

It had been a long, painful and lonely labor. There were two other women in the labor room with her and both had been panting and puffing in great Lamaze style with supportive husbands at their sides. Susan had suffered in silence and alone.

Ricardo had never even suggested that he might be present when the baby was born. The thought, she had come to realize, simply never crossed his mind. Childbirth, in his view, was woman's work. After two months she had come to learn a few things about the man she had married and one thing had become increasingly clear. He was *not* a liberated male.

He must have been waiting at the hospital, though, because he came into see her as soon as she was brought back from the delivery room. He came across to the bed immediately and picked up her hand. "How are you feeling, *querida?*" he asked softly.

"Tired." She gazed up at him gravely. His hair was

tousled and the shadow of his beard was dark and rough. He looked tired, too, she thought.

"It took a long time," he said.

"You're telling me," she answered, and at that he smiled at her, not the quick irrepressible grin that so beguiled strangers but a slow, warm, intimate smile that lit his extraordinary eyes as if from within. Her own face softened and for a brief moment the weariness disappeared. She smiled back, a bewitchingly beautiful smile. "Have you see him yet?" she asked.

"No. I'll stop by the nursery on my way out. I wanted to see you first." Susan felt an unaccountable stab of joy when he said those words. "The doctor wanted me to come into the delivery room," he was going on, a note of horror in his voice. "Can you imagine? He seemed very put out when I said no."

The look on his face made her giggle. "A lot of husbands do, you know."

"A lot of husbands are crazy," he said firmly. He bent to kiss her gently. "Get some rest, *querida*. I'll see you later."

He had reached the door before she thought to call, "Did you win?"

"What? Oh." He turned and grinned. "We did, one to nothing. I hit a home run. Good night, Susan."

"Good night, Ricardo," she answered softly, and looked for a long time at the empty doorway before she closed her eyes and fell asleep.

Two days after his son was born, Ricardo flew to Los Angeles for the opening game of the World Series. Susan watched the game on TV in her hospital room. The Yankees lost, 5–4, in extra innings. Ricardo had singled twice and doubled.

The next day Mrs. Morgan came down to Stamford

and brought Susan and the baby home from the hospital. She was clearly entranced by her grandson and talked enthusiastically about the play-offs and last night's game. Susan stared at her mother in astonishment. To her knowledge, Mrs. Morgan had never watched a baseball game in her life.

Maria, Ricardo's maid, was almost as ecstatic about the baby as his grandmother, and before she could say a word, Susan found herself being tucked up in bed while her son was kept downstairs in his port-a-crib, vigilantly guarded by two doting would-be nannies. At first she was a little annoyed—he was *her* son, after all. But then her sense of humor reasserted itself. She'd get him back fast enough when he was hungry. In that respect, he was remarkably like his father!

The Yankees lost the second game in Los Angeles as well, 4–3, after holding a 3–1 lead until the ninth inning. The game was over at eleven P.M. Los Angeles time, and immediately afterward the team got a plane back to New York. Consequently, Ricardo arrived home at ten o'clock the following morning without having been to bed. Susan was bathing the baby in the sunny bedroom she had made into a nursery when he walked in the door. He stood for a minute in silence, watching her deft, gentle hands manipulate the squalling infant. Then, although he had made no sound, her head swung around and she saw him. Her gray eyes widened. "Ricardo! You're back."

"I'm back." He came into the room and regarded his son in some astonishment.

Susan laughed. "He's not overly fond of water." She scooped the baby up, wrapped him in a hooded towel and handed him to his father.

"*Dios!*" said Ricardo, startled and clearly uneasy. "He's awfully small."

"Actually, he's rather large. Nine pounds, as I remember to my sorrow."

Ricardo began to rock the baby and the crying stopped. His eyes sparkled as he looked at Susan. "I think I am a natural," he said. He looked so extremely proud of himself that Susan had to stifle a giggle.

"Make sure you support his head," she said. "Here. Like this." Ricardo's strong brown hand was larger than the baby's head but he was cradling the child with instinctive tenderness. Susan felt her eyes mist over and she blinked hard. "Say hello to your father," he was saying to the small face of his son, and Susan had to blink again.

Ricardo slept for a few hours and then in the afternoon he raked some leaves. "I'll have to have a pool put in," he said over dinner. "I never did before because I was gone half the time and there was no one to look after it."

Susan felt a flash of irritation. "And now you have a wife to take care of it for you."

"Yes." He smiled at her serenely. "Wouldn't you like a pool?"

She would, of course. She just didn't like to be regarded in such a utilitarian manner. "Yes," she said a little unwillingly. "I suppose a pool would be nice."

"I'll see about it."

"All right." She hoped, belatedly, that she had not sounded sulky.

They went to bed early, as both of them were decidedly short of sleep. Susan had the baby in a bassinet in her room so she could hear him when he awoke, which he did promptly at midnight. She picked him up and was preparing to sit down in the chair to nurse him when her door opened and Ricardo appeared. "What's the matter?" he asked. "I heard the baby crying."

Susan looked up at the tall figure of her husband. He was wearing only a pair of pajama bottoms and she stared for a moment in wonder at the great muscles of his chest and biceps and shoulders. She looked up further and met his eyes. Without her shoes, the top of her head reached barely to his shoulder. "He's hungry, that's all," she said in what she hoped was a calm voice. "He needs to nurse every four hours."

"Oh. I was afraid he was sick or something."

"No. It's nothing like that." She sat down in the chair and hesitated for a moment. He hadn't moved and she found herself reluctant to nurse the baby in front of him. Slowly she unbuttoned the front of her nightgown and put the baby to her breast. The crying stopped instantly. She glanced at Ricardo. He was staring at his son, looking absolutely fascinated. "You'd better get some sleep," she said. "You have a game this afternoon."

"That's true." He moved to the door with obvious reluctance. "Good night, *querida*."

"Good night," she answered softly.

The Yankees opened in New York at two o'clock that afternoon, two games down in a series where one team had to win four games in order to take the championship. It was essential, Ricardo had told Susan, that they win all three games in their home ball park. The last two games would be played at Dodger Stadium in Los Angeles.

The baby was sleeping peacefully when Susan and Maria Martinez sat down in front of the TV. The stadium was packed with over sixty thousand fans, the announcer informed them. As the camera panned around the park all one could see was an unending sea of faces: old and young, male and female, rich and poor, all smiling and waving and brandishing signs.

The Dodger team was introduced first, drawing mixed applause and boos from the New York fans. Then it was the turn of the home team. "Batting first and playing second base, Joe Hutchinson," the loudspeaker boomed. Applause swept over the ball park as the first three men came out of the dugout and onto the grass. Then, "Batting fourth and playing center field," the announcer said and a roar went up from sixty-thousand throats. *"Rick Montoya,"* the announcer shouted into the microphone, and Susan watched her husband jog onto the field and shake the hands of his teammates. The uproar showed absolutely no signs of subsiding and Ricardo tipped his cap in acknowledgment. Good God, Susan thought in stunned amazement, I had no idea it would be like this.

The crowd finally quieted enough for the rest of the team to be introduced and then the Yankees took the field and a famous opera singer sang "The Star Spangled Banner." An illustrious old Yankee player threw out the first ball and the game began.

It was the kind of game baseball fanatics dream of. The lead changed hands twice, and going into the ninth inning the score was 6–5, Yankees. The first Dodger up hit a home run and the score was tied. The next man singled and the Yankee manager brought in a new pitcher. The next two men flied out and then Frank Revere stepped up to the plate. Revere had forty home runs to his credit during the regular season and with the *crack* sound of the bat on the first pitch, Susan thought he had notched number forty-one.

Then the camera picked up Ricardo in center field. He was back against the wall and at the very last instant he leaped, impossibly, dangerously high, and the ball landed in the webbing of his glove. The ball park exploded into pandemonium.

"What a catch!" the announcer was shrieking over the bedlam. "I don't believe I saw that!"

"I don't believe it either," Susan said a little numbly. Maria was screaming at the television in Spanish and Susan turned to her with a grin. "Ditto for me," she said, and laughed.

The Yankees came to the plate in the bottom of the ninth with the score tied. The leadoff man singled, but then Buddy Moran hit a hard line drive right at the first baseman and the Dodgers made a double play. When Ricardo walked up to the plate, Susan thought the stadium had gone mad. Her palms and her forehead were damp with sweat. My God, she thought, how is it possible for anyone to perform under that kind of pressure? Her stomach heaved and she felt slightly sick.

Ricardo swung his bat with the even, elegant, iron-wristed swing that had become so familiar to her over the last two months. He looked intent and very serious in the close-up camera shot. Knocking the dirt out of his spikes, he stepped up to the plate.

The count ran out to 3 and 2 and Susan's feeling of nausea increased uncomfortably. I can't stand this, she was thinking as the pitcher went into his windup. Ricardo swung.

"That's it!" the announcer shouted. "That's the ball game!"

And indeed it was. As sixty-thousand hysterical and

delirious fans pounded each other on the back and
threw things onto the field in their ecstasy, Ricardo
jogged around the bases, a huge grin on his face.
There had never been any doubt about that ball being
caught; it had landed far back in the upper left-field
grandstand.

The Yankees won the next two games in New
York as well and then they returned to Los Angeles,
ahead of the Dodgers three games to two. Susan felt
that her whole life was divided between taking care
of the baby and watching baseball. One of the things
that struck her as she watched the games was the
way the television camera would zero in on the faces
of the players' wives. She was very glad she had the
excuse of a nursing infant to keep from attending in
person. She would hate to be singled out like that,
broadcasted and exposed. It was bad enough
watching at home.

They lost the first game in Los Angeles, 7–6. In the
second game, the game on which the championship
depended, the score was tied in the ninth, 4–4, and
the game went into extra innings. The Yankees' relief
pitcher, Sal Fatato, got into trouble in the top of the
eleventh inning and only got out of it when Ricardo
threw a perfect strike all the way from center field to
cut down Frank Revere. In the bottom of the eleventh, Joe Hutchinson singled, moved to second on a
sacrifice and Ricardo doubled him home. The Yankees were the new World Champions.

"This World Series was finally won," wrote noted
sports columnist Frank Winter in the *New York Times*
the next day, "by the hitting, the throwing, the
fielding, the sheer blazing brilliance of Rick Montoya.
Rarely has a World Series Most Valuable Player
Award been more thoroughly deserved."

"Congratulations," Susan said when Ricardo arrived home the following day. "I almost had heart failure half a dozen times and Maria was even worse. Couldn't you have won in a less *dramatic* fashion?"

He grinned. "It wouldn't have been as much fun."

"Fun," Susan said faintly. She thought of the dreadful pressure of all those screaming fans. "You call that fun?"

"Absolutely."

"Oh, Señor Montoya," came a high-pitched voice from behind Susan, and Ricardo laughed.

"Oh, Maria," he mimicked, and catching her in his arms, he kissed her soundly. Maria's worn face glowed with pleasure. Ricardo had not kissed his wife. "Where's my son?" he asked.

"Upstairs asleep," she answered slowly.

"I won't wake him, then." He took off his jacket and threw it on a chair. Maria hurried to pick it up. "Did the paper come?" he asked.

"Si, Señor Montoya." Maria picked the *Times* up from a table and handed it to him. Ricardo sat down in a comfortable chair, stretched his long legs in front of him and opened the paper. "I'll have some coffee," he said from behind the sports page.

"Sí, Señor Montoya," said Maria again, and disappeared in the direction of the kitchen.

Susan stood in the middle of the room and stared at the paper that concealed her husband. The baseball season was over, she thought, and here he was—home until spring. Maria returned with the coffee, which she set on a table at his elbow. He grunted a thank you. Quite suddenly she was furious.

"Perhaps if I knelt down in front of you, you could

rest your feet on my back," she said in a voice she had never used with him.

He lowered his paper and stared at her in astonishment. "What did you say, *querida*?"

"You heard me." She stared back at him steadily, clear gray eyes like slate under the surprisingly dark and level brows.

"But why are you angry?" he asked in genuine bewilderment.

"You're so wonderful," she said acidly. "You figure it out." And she stalked from the room.

Chapter Five

A week after the World Series was won, the Yankees' owner threw a dinner party for his team. It was held at a very elegant New York hotel and Ricardo told Susan he expected her to attend with him.

"But I can't leave the baby," she protested feebly.

"Nonsense. Maria will stay with him for the evening. I'll drive her home when we get back."

"But what if he gets hungry?"

"He can drink a bottle. Or he can wait." He cocked an eyebrow. "You don't want me to invite someone else, do you, *querida?*"

Susan lifted her chin. "I'll come," she said.

"Good." He smiled at her engagingly, willing her to be pleased. "You'll have a good time. You need to get out more."

It wasn't that she wouldn't enjoy going out to dinner, Susan thought as she went through her wardrobe in search of something to wear. It was just that she quailed at the thought of meeting all those people who knew, who *had* to know, that she and Ricardo had been married only two months before Ricky was born.

She closed the closet door on her schoolgirl clothes and went over to look down into the bassinet at her sleeping son. Ricky's face, she thought with a flicker of extreme tenderness, was the surest proof of his paternity. He was a miniature of his father. Not that Ricardo had ever, in any way at all, even hinted that he might wonder if the baby she had been carrying was really his. She had always felt immensely grateful to him for that trust. She still did. It was one of the things she always remembered when she found his lordly masculinity getting on her nerves. He had believed her word, and on the basis of that word he had married her. She doubted there were many men—particularly men in his position—who would have done the same.

She settled a light cover on her sleeping son and sighed. She would have to buy a dress. And have Sara's black coat altered. Her old camel hair would not do for the St. Regis. She was going to have to talk to Ricardo about money.

Ever since she had come to live with him, Ricardo had continued the same financial arrangements he had always had. He gave Maria a housekeeping allowance and out of it she bought the groceries and took care of the laundry and the dry cleaning. Over and above that, of course, she got her salary. A salary that was extremely generous, Susan realized, when Maria told her what it amounted to. Ricardo had also bought his housekeeper a car so she could drive from her home in Norwalk to his in Stamford and so that she could do the errands. Maria thought that God was simply another name for Ricardo.

He certainly had never grudged his wife money either, but Susan didn't enjoy playing the beggar maid to his King Cophetua. The purchases she had made—which consisted mainly of furniture and clothing for the baby—he had agreed to immediately and generously. "How much do you want, *querida*?" he would say, and unhesitatingly hand over to her the amount she requested. The problem was, she hated having to ask.

She hated having to talk to him about this, too, but it was going to have to be done. She arrived downstairs just as he was coming in from raking leaves. "*Dios!*" he said to her humorously. "I think half the leaves in Connecticut have found a home in my yard. The more I rake, the more leaves there seem to be. At least I can dump them in the woods. I'd hate to have to bag them all."

"We used to burn them," Susan said nostalgically. "I loved the smell of leaves burning in the fall. It seemed like such a big part of the season."

"Well, if I burn them now I will get a summons," Ricardo said practically. He took off his down vest and dropped it on a chair.

"Ricardo," Susan said with exemplary patience, "there is a closet right behind you. Do you think you could hang that up?"

He looked surprised. "It doesn't go in that closet," he said simply. "It goes upstairs."

There was a short silence and then Susan decided to fight this particular battle another day. She cleared her throat. "I have to talk to you, Ricardo. Could we sit down for a minute, please?"

"Of course." He followed her into the family room. There was a chill in the air and he said, "I think we could use a fire."

She sat down on the sofa and watched as he expertly stacked wood in the stone fireplace. The shoulders under his plaid flannel shirt looked so wide, so strong, so—impervious. Could she possibly make him understand how she felt? He sat back on his heels

and watched as the fire grew. Then he turned and
looked at her. "So?" he said. "What do you want to
talk to me about?"

"Well—I need a dress for the dinner on Saturday,
for one thing," she began.

"Naturally." He sounded surprised that she should
need to mention this obvious fact.

"Ricardo," and now her voice began to sound
tense, "can't you see that I hate to have to come and
ask you every time I need money? It isn't that you
aren't generous—you're only too generous—it's just
that, well, it's just that I hate it." She looked at him a
little desperately, a mute appeal in her large gray
eyes.

He looked back at her and his own face became very
grave. "Susan," he said, "forgive me. Of course you
should not have to come and ask me for every penny.
I am sorry. I should have made you an allowance long
ago." He gave her a faintly rueful, utterly charming
look. "I was preoccupied with other things," he said.
"Shall I give you a monthly allowance for you and for
Ricky? How about . . ." and he named a sum that
made her blink.

And that was it. It had been so easy. He had, surprisingly, understood. "Thank you, Ricardo," she said
a little breathlessly. "Honestly, I don't mean to be a
millstone around your neck forever, but I am rather
tied down with the baby at present. I just don't think I
can get a job right now."

"A job!" He looked utterly thunderstruck. "What
are you talking about, Susan? You are not a millstone
around my neck. You are my wife. The mother of my
son. Of course I expect to support you. I won't hear of
you getting a job."

She stared back at him, startled by his vehemence,

even more startled by his point of view. Her own mother had always worked outside the home. She herself had always assumed that was what educated women did. "Not now, of course, while Ricky is still little," she began tentatively.

"Not now, not ever," he said firmly. "You have a job. You are a wife and a mother. You are a very good mother, *querida*. I always knew you would be. And we will have more children. You'll be busy enough, I promise you."

Susan felt her heart lurch a little at that mention of more children. She ran her tongue around suddenly dry lips. "Ricardo." She spoke very gently, very carefully, "I am twenty-two years old. I have a college degree. I had—I have—plans for my life that involve something more than being just a housewife."

Ricardo's mouth set in a line that was not at all gentle. "And what are these plans?" he asked in an abrupt, hard voice.

"Well," said Susan weakly, pushed to the wall and forced to admit out loud and to someone else what she had scarcely dared admit to herself, "I've always wanted to be a writer."

The set of his mouth got even grimmer. "On a newspaper?"

"No. Oh, no. I've wanted to write—novels." The last word came out as barely a whisper. She was desperately afraid that he would laugh.

His face relaxed but he did not laugh. "Oh novels," he said. He smiled at her, his good humor restored. "I have no objection to your writing novels, *querida*. That is something you can easily do at home."

"Yes, I suppose I could," she said slowly.

"We even have a library for you to work in," he said magnanimously.

She stared at his splendid dark face. He was humoring her, she thought. He did not take her at all seriously. "Thank you," she said, her voice expressionless.

"Not at all." He waved his hand in a gesture of magnificent dismissal. "And what is all this foolishness about being 'just a housewife.' You aren't a housewife, you're *my* wife." His eyes glinted at her and his voice became softer. "I realize we have been somewhat delayed in starting a normal married life," he went on, "but that should be over with soon. When do you see the doctor again?"

She could hear her heart hammering way up into her head. "In three weeks," she got out.

"So long. Ah well." He leaned back in the armchair and closed his eyes. "I've waited this long. I suppose another three weeks won't kill me." There was absolute silence in the room. Susan couldn't think of a thing to say. He opened his eyes a slit. "I'm thirsty after all that raking. Could you get me something to drink?"

It was definitely not the time to take up a feminist stance. Susan stood up. "What do you want?"

"Some ginger ale would be nice."

She nodded and left the room, shaking her head ruefully.

The dinner party turned out to be a very enjoyable evening. Susan had bought a pale gold dinner dress in Bloomingdale's and was conscious of looking really smart for the first time in almost a year. Her shining, fawn-colored hair, so fine that it wouldn't hold a curl, fell, sheer and glistening to her shoulders. She wore high-heeled gold sandals and Sara's black coat and she felt pretty as well as smart. It didn't hurt either, she thought as they went in through the doors of the hotel, to have an escort as impressive-looking as Ricardo. Even if he had never played baseball in his life, his tall, broad-shouldered figure would have commanded attention.

It was the first time that Susan had ever met any of Ricardo's teammates, with the exception of Joe Hutchinson, and it was fun actually seeing in person the people she had been watching so assiduously on TV. They sat at a table with Joe Hutchinson, Bert Diaz, Carl Seelinger and their wives. The conversation, after the first few minutes, drifted away from baseball and Susan found herself talking to the quiet, shy wife of Bert Diaz. Sonia Diaz's English was halting, so Susan, who had been getting in a lot of practice with Maria, spoke with her in Spanish. The Diazes had a six-month-old daughter, and the two women happily talked babies during the appetizer and soup courses. Susan's attention was wrested from this fascinating topic, however, when she heard Carl Seelinger ask Ricardo, "And what are you going to do this winter, Rick? If you do any more skiing, George will have a heart attack. He does not want you reporting to spring training with a broken leg."

Ricardo looked amused. "George is a worry wart." He sipped his wine. "We'll be leaving for Bogotá before long. I don't want to delay Ricky's christening forever and my mother and sisters are dying to see him."

"Are you having the baby christened in Colombia, Rick?" asked Jane Hutchinson.

"Of course. That's where my family is."

All of this was news to Susan. They hadn't even discussed the subject of Ricky's baptism. Susan had assumed that Ricardo would want him baptized Catholic and she didn't plan to object. She herself was Congregational, but her family had never been churchgoers. She hadn't noticed that Ricardo was much of a churchgoer, either, but he had made a point of their being married by a priest.

He might also have made a point of discussing his plans with her, she thought now as she watched his oblivious profile. Her chest felt tight, the way it always did when she was upset. "You never told me we were taking Ricky to Colombia," she said in a low voice to him a little later in the meal.

He looked surprised. "Of course I did, *querida*. I said we would go to Bogotá for Christmas. Don't you remember?"

"For Christmas. Not for a christening."

He shrugged and gave her his charming, boyish smile. She was getting to know his expressions very well. This one meant, Oh well, I didn't think it was important, but if you want to make an issue of it, I'll humor you. "I didn't think it mattered to you," he said patiently. "Would you like your mother to be there? I'll give her airplane tickets."

That wasn't the issue at all. The issue was that she wanted to be consulted before plans were made that involved her and her baby. It wasn't that she objected to Ricardo's plan; she just wanted to be part of the decision-making process.

"That's not it," she said softly. "We'll talk about it later, at home."

He looked a little surprised but then his attention was claimed again by Jane Hutchinson. In a few minutes the conversation had become general.

"You're different from the girls Rick used to date," Bev Seelinger said to Susan as they fresheneed their makeup in the ladies' room after dinner. "Somehow I knew you would be."

Susan fought a brief battle with herself and lost. "What kind of girls did he date?" she asked.

"Oh, the tall, sultry model type. But I never for a minute thought he'd marry any of them. In fact, I sometimes wondered if he'd ever marry at all."

Susan put her comb down and looked curiously at her companion. "Why?"

"I don't know," the other woman answered slowly. She flashed Susan a quick grin. "It's not that he doesn't like women. God, when I remember how those model types used to be all over him." Bev frowned. "It's odd, now I come to think of it, that I never pictured him as married."

"Perhaps he was too much the playboy type," Susan said with an effort at lightness. She felt guilty discussing Ricardo like this. She felt almost that she was betraying his privacy. But she couldn't help herself. She knew so little, even now, about this man she had married.

"No," Bev was saying decisively. "That's not it. He certainly had a lot of girlfriends, and he certainly has a sex appeal that would knock over your eighty-year-old maiden aunt if he turned it on her, but that's not it. It's just that—somehow, one always sees Rick as essentially alone."

Susan stared at Bev's healthy, outdoor face. It was not the face of a deeply perceptive woman but, Susan suddenly realized, that was what she was. "Yes," she said softly after a minute, "I know what you mean."

Bev smiled at her gratefully. "I don't know what got me started on this topic. I hope you don't feel I've been out of line."

"No, of course I don't." Susan put her comb back in her purse. "Are you ready? Shall we go?"

Susan thought about what Bev had said as the evening progressed to after-dinner drinks and a three-piece band for dancing. As she had watched the World Series on TV and read the ecstatic press reports, she had tried to comprehend, to analyze, the astonishing popularity of her husband. It was not just his baseball talent—other men were equally talented, she thought. It was something about him, something inherent in his character, that made him what he was: Rick Montoya, American idol.

She watched him now, relaxed and laughing among his teammates, and even here he stood out. He was one of them but he was still, always and incontestably, his own man, invincibly private behind all the outward good cheer. Susan, always deeply sensitive to the vibrations of another spirit, had long apprehended this solitariness in her husband. It was the thing in him that most frustrated and fascinated her.

"Dance with me?" Ricardo's voice broke into her reverie and she looked up into his dark eyes.

"Of course."

He took her hand and they moved out onto the floor. The band was playing "Moon River," and Ricardo's arms came around her and held her close. She had not been this close to him since that night in the blizzard, the night Ricky had been conceived. His body felt so strong against hers, so big. The music was slow and dreamy and she relaxed against him, supple and light, following his slightest move effortlessly. When the song was over he looked down at her, his eyes warm and very dark. "That was nice," he said softly. She didn't answer and the band began another slow song. "Again?" he asked, and she nodded and moved back into his arms. "What a shame we have to wait three more weeks," he murmured against the silky softness of her hair. And at that moment, seduced by the intense magnetism of his nearness, Susan had to agree.

Chapter Six

❧

"I don't know what's the matter with me," Susan wrote in her journal one evening two weeks after the dinner in New York, "but I can't seem to organize my life and get down to writing anything. There's no excuse, really. Maria does the housework and a great deal of the cooking. I only have the baby to deal with. But somehow there never seems to be any *time*."

She sighed and looked out the window. The main problem, she thought, was Ricardo. He had spent the last few weeks building shelves in the baby's room and he had had the foundation poured for an addition to the garage. He had come home a week ago with a new Volvo station wagon for her, which needed garage space as the present two-car garage housed Ricardo's Mercedes and the new sports car he had won as MVP of the World Series. When they got back from Bogotá he was going to have the new garage addition framed out and then he would finish it himself.

All of these were Ricardo's projects but they seemed to eat incessantly into Susan's time. He needed someone to hold his hammer, to hold a board straight, to run to the store for sandpaper. She had to drive the new Volvo over half of Connecticut before he was satisfied she was competent to handle it alone. She wondered sometimes if it wasn't his strategy to keep her so occupied that there wasn't room in her life for anything else.

"The problem is," she wrote reflectively, "that I don't feel confident enough to demand time for myself. Who am I to say I'm a writer? Who am I to say I need time away from my husband, my child? Who am I—a mediocre scholar, a shotgun wife—to make any kind of demand of Ricardo? And yet—I feel I *must* make it, that if I don't, I'll suffocate."

She was sitting at the desk in her bedroom and now the lights of a car caught her attention as they swung into the drive. Ricardo was home.

Ricardo was home and she would go downstairs to greet him, to ask him about his dinner, about his speech, about the people he had seen. He would smile at her good-naturedly, that famous ingratiating grin that had charmed millions, and shortly afterward she would go to bed in her own private room.

Next week, of course, she would see the doctor and all of that would change.

It frightened her, the prospect of sleeping with him again. He had seemed so confident these last two weeks, so toughly competent in all his undertakings, so calmly dominant where she was concerned. And yet he scarcely touched her, never kissed her. She didn't like to admit it, but she was afraid of him. She was afraid, inexplicably, of his maleness, his capability, his way of "dealing" with her. When the time came he would take her to bed with the same casual expertise with which he did everything else. He would impose his own implacable reality upon the hazy memory of that night in New Hampshire, and she was afraid he would destroy it. For some peculiar reason she was unable to associate the Ricardo she knew with the Ricardo of that night. They seemed two separate

and distinct people. She felt as if she would be going
to bed with a stranger.

"You're just fine, Mrs. Montoya," the doctor told
her reassuringly. "You can resume sex without any
problem. Would you like me to give you a prescription for birth-control pills?"

Susan said yes and then had the prescription filled
before she drove home. She also stopped at Lord and
Taylor and did a little shopping. Ricardo was speaking at a Little League sports dinner that evening and
Susan wanted him to be gone before she arrived
home, so she delayed for as long as she could.

She was successful; the sports car was gone when
she peeked into the garage before going into the
house. Maria was waiting, ready to go home, and
Ricky was indignant because his dinner had been
delayed.

It was a very long night. Susan fed Ricky and put
him to bed, then, knowing it would be impossible for
her to write, she switched on the TV. At eleven she
fed Ricky once again, took a shower and got into bed.
Her room seemed very large and very strange. They
had moved the baby's crib into the nursery a few days
ago and she was alone. She closed her eyes and tried
to go to sleep, but all her muscles were tense with waiting. At twelve-thirty she heard the sound of Ricardo's
car on the drive.

It seemed forever before his feet sounded on the
stairs. Then the door to her room opened and closed
and Ricardo was standing there, his shoulders against
it, motionless in the dim glow from the night-light
Susan kept burning so she could see if she had to get
up with the baby. His face was shadowed and he did
not speak—or maybe it was that she could not hear

him above the thudding of her heart. Then he came across the room and stood, towering, next to the bed. He said her name.

"Yes?" She hoped, desperately, that she sounded sleepy. "What do you want, Ricardo?"

"Really, Susan, what a question." He sounded amused.

She was aware of him standing there with every pore of her body. "How was your dinner?" she asked, and sat up, pushing her hair out of her face.

"I don't want to talk about my dinner," he said softly, and sat down on the bed next to her. "How did your checkup go?"

"All right." Her voice sounded squeaky in her own ears. "He said I'm okay."

"Now that is very good news." He raised a hand and lifted the hair from her neck. "It's been a very long wait," he said, and let the pale silky strands slide through his fingers.

"Ricardo." She moistened her lips with her tongue. "It's been a long day and I'm tired. Perhaps we could wait. . . ."

Her voice trailed off. He was taking off his suit jacket and undoing his tie. "No, *querida*," he said. "We can't wait." He dropped the jacket and tie on the floor and started in on the buttons of his blue dress shirt. In a minute the shirt had followed the rest of his clothes to the floor.

"They'll get all wrinkled," Susan croaked out of a dry throat. His bare chest and shoulders looked enormous in the dim light of her bedroom.

"It doesn't matter," he answered impatiently, and began to unbuckle his belt. Susan shivered and dragged her eyes away from him. She was breathing very quickly.

I'm being stupid, she told herself. It will be wonderful, just as it was the first time. The bed creaked as it took the brunt of his weight and her eyes flew up to his face. For the first time he seemed to apprehend that something was wrong.

"Susan," he said. *"Querida."* His voice was deep, caressing. "You aren't afraid of me?"

It was the voice of the blizzard. "Ricardo," she said uncertainly, and he answered, "Shh, little one. It will be all right." And he bent his head and kissed her.

It was an infinitely gentle kiss, infinitely sweet. After a moment he eased her back against the mattress and stretched out beside her, gathering her close against him. She remembered instantly the feel of his body and slowly her arms curved up to hold him. "Susan," he said in her ear. His mouth brushed her cheek, her temple. *"Dios,* but it has been a long wait."

She arched her head back to look up at him. "Did you mind?" she asked wonderingly.

He made a sound deep down in his throat. "I am a man," he said. "Of course I minded."

"Oh," breathed Susan, and then he kissed her again. Her lips softened under his and immediately the kiss became more forceful, his mouth opening hungrily on hers in an erotic demand she recognized and involuntarily surrendered to.

It was like nothing else in the world, the feel of Ricardo's rough calloused hands, so incredibly sure and delicate on her body. She melted before the magic of it, opening for him as a flower opens to the warmth of the sun. He seemed to sense the magnitude of her surrender, for his gentle caresses became something more. She had the dizzy feeling of being violently overthrown and mastered, and then, astonishing, her own passion came beating up, answering strongly to his, overwhelming and all-encompassing. When it was over they lay still, locked together, not ready yet to return to their separate identities.

It was he who spoke first. "Do you know why I never tried to see you after that night in New Hampshire?"

His breath lightly stirred the silky hair on her temple. His voice was so soft, so deep, it penetrated her nerves. "No," she answered on a bare breath of sound.

"It was because I didn't want to spoil the memory of that night, and I was afraid that if we met again it would never seem the same." He chuckled. "It was rather like something out of a medieval romance, you must admit: the night, the storm, the beautiful young virgin."

She had never suspected him capable of such profound romanticism. "I know," she whispered. "It was—you said it was magic."

"It was." He rubbed his cheek against her hair. "I expected you to turn into a unicorn the next morning and gallop off into the mountains."

She sighed. "And instead I turned into a very pregnant lady whom you had to marry."

"Well, let us say rather you turned into a very pregnant unicorn," he suggested, and she giggled. "But I'm not sorry we got married," he was going on. "Are you?"

She was acutely conscious of his nearness, his maleness, his power and strength. He was the biggest thing that had ever happened to her. She knew that and she knew, too, in a sudden flash of intuition, that he always would be. Nothing else in her life would ever measure up to the importance of Ricardo. "No," she said, low and steady, "no, I'm not sorry."

"Good." He burrowed comfortably deeper into the

bed and in two minutes he was asleep. Susan lay awake for much much longer before she finally drifted into a dreamless slumber.

The next few weeks slipped by for Susan, heavy with the haze of sensual fulfillment. All the minor discontents and irritations of the past weeks seemed simply to vanish. Her world both expanded and contracted and that world consisted of just one thing: Ricardo. Even the baby became somehow an extension of her husband. All of Susan's intellectuality and feminism died, drowned in the absorbing, purely physical life she was leading. For the first time in her life she was profoundly conscious of the pleasures of being female. She wrote absolutely nothing.

"I got our tickets for Bogotá today," Ricardo said to her one evening in early December. They were sitting in the family room in front of the fire, Susan curled up on the sofa next to Ricardo, her head pillowed against the hardness of his shoulder. She stirred a little and looked up at him.

"What?"

"I got our tickets for Bogotá. We leave in four days."

She sat up and stared at him. The glow from the fire cast golden shadows on his warm olive skin and high cheekbones. "Four days?" she repeated.

"Um." He looked at her and quite suddenly frowned. "You did update your passport, as I asked?"

She had done that months ago. "Yes. But, Ricardo, four days! I have to pack and get Ricky ready . . . Ricky! He doesn't have a passport!"

"Oh yes, he does. I got him one a month ago."

"You got him one. . . . But when?"

He looked a little impatient. "I had the photographer come to the house. Don't you remember?"

"No." She was quite definite. "I do not remember."

He looked even more impatient. "Well, perhaps you weren't home. As a matter of fact, now that I think of it, you were out getting your hair cut."

She stared at him, utterly flabbergasted. "And you didn't even think to tell me?"

He shrugged. "I forgot." He raised an eyebrow. "But what is all this fuss, *querida*? Ricky has a passport. You have a passport. I am so important that I have *two* passports. You throw some clothes into a suitcase, and we go. Why are you upsetting yourself?"

She expelled her breath in a sound of mingled exasperation and defeat. "I don't know. I suppose it's utterly weird of me, but I *would* like to be kept a little more apprised of your plans for us, Ricardo."

He looked surprised. "Don't you want to go?"

"Of course I want to go." She looked up at his splendidly masculine face and surrendered. "Why do you have two passports?" she asked.

He smiled, irresistible and charming now that she had given way to him. "I have both a Colombian passport and an American passport. When I am traveling to Colombia I use one and when I am returning to the States I use the other."

"How convenient."

"Isn't it?" He looked down at her. "But then, I have always liked convenience. I find having a wife is very convenient. If I had known how much I would like it, I might have married years ago. Aren't you lucky I waited?" He picked up her hand, turned it slightly and kissed first her wrist and then her palm.

"You mightn't have found another wife quite as

convenient as I am," she said very softly. The touch of his mouth was causing her heartbeat to accelerate.

"That is true." He shifted his grasp to her wrist and pulled her closer to him. "Let's make love right here, in front of the fire," he murmured.

Susan's eyes widened with surprise. "Here?"

"Here." He bent his head and began to kiss her, slowly, seekingly, erotically. He pressed her back against the cushions of the sofa and her hands came up to hold him. The muscles of his back and shoulders were hard under her palms. He kissed her throat, her collarbone, and his hand moved up under her sweater toward her breast.

"Ricardo," she whispered. She kissed his cheekbone, his ear. "Let's go upstairs."

"No," he said. "Here." His fingers found her breast and his other hand began to move caressingly along her hip, her thigh. Susan's body responded even as her mind hesitated, her New England conservatism slightly scandalized by his behavior. This wasn't a ski chalet in New Hampshire; this was her home.

He sensed her indecision and pulled back a little to look into her face. He was so close he could clearly see the baby-fine texture of her skin. Her wide gray eyes were both unsure and voluptuous, her mouth was so soft, so inviting. . . . "Little puritan," he said, and then his weight bore her back against the wide cushions of the sofa.

"Ricardo . . ." Susan said protestingly, but her hands closed on his shoulders and held him close.

"*Cariña,*" he said. "*Angelita.*" Susan's eyelids felt heavy as her body ripened under his touch. She helped him take off her clothes, conscious at last only of the rushing of her blood, the sweet melting desire that longed for him to take her and make her his. The fire was hot on her bare skin and he was deep within her. Her whole body shuddered with the intensity of the pleasure he gave her and she buried her face, her mouth, in the sweaty hollow of his shoulder. She said his name, and then she said it again. He rolled over onto his side, still keeping his arms around her, and they lay still. After a long while Susan raised her head and, bending, rained a line of tender kisses along his face, from temple to chin. Her hair swung forward, enclosing both their faces in a silken tent. She raised her head a little and he smiled at her, warm and peaceful in the glow of the fire. Later he carried her upstairs to bed.

Susan spent the next three days doing laundry and packing. On the day before they were to leave she put Ricky in his car seat and drove up to Fairfield to visit her mother.

"Why don't you come to Bogotá for your Christmas vacation, Mother?" she asked as they sat over a cup of coffee in the kitchen. Ricky was sleeping next to them in the port-a-crib Susan had brought along with her.

"I'd love to, dear, but I'm afraid I won't be able to," Mrs. Morgan said. "There's a whole calendar full of dinners and parties I've promised to attend."

"But what will you do on Christmas?"

"The Slatterlys have asked me for the day." Anne Slatterly was an old college friend of her mother's and the two had always remained very close.

"Oh," said Susan. She smiled and said lightly, "I can see I don't have to worry about your being alone."

"Of course not." Mrs. Morgan smiled down at her sleeping grandson. "I'll miss this little guy, though."

"Yes. Well, we'll be back sometime after the first of the year."

"When exactly are you coming home, Susan? I forgot to ask you the other day."

"I don't know." Susan sipped her coffee. "Ricardo hasn't said. But I'll call you when we get in."

Amusement lit Mrs. Morgan's face. "Ricardo doesn't know how lucky he was to marry you, Susan. There are very few American girls today who would be as accommodating to his 'lord of the manor' style as you."

Susan kept her eyes on her coffee. She tried very hard not to feel hurt, but she was. "That's just the way he is," she managed to say.

"I know. And you are—and always have been—a sweet, gentle and affectionate child. You'll suit him perfectly." Mrs. Morgan got up to take a coffee cake out of the oven. "What is Ricardo doing these days to keep himself busy?" she asked as she served her daughter a slice.

"He's been going into New York these last few days, to film a camera commercial for television."

"Oh? Good for him. There's a great deal of money to be made in that sort of thing. Does he do it often?"

"Once in a while. For products he really uses and likes."

"And what have you been up to, dear?"

"Well," Susan said feebly, "the baby keeps me busy." She looked down at her sleeping son. He didn't look as if he kept anyone busy.

"But you have Maria to help?" Her mother was prodding gently.

"That's true."

"You ought to join a few local organizations," Mrs. Morgan advised. "Stamford has some excellent civic groups." Mrs. Morgan herself was a member of various professional, political and civic organizations.

All her life Susan could recall her mother going out to meetings.

"I'll think about it," Susan said with noticeable lack of enthusiasm. Her mother gave her a slightly baffled look and then, obligingly, changed the subject.

Driving herself home an hour later, Susan felt the old familiar sense of worthlessness sweep across her. She was bitterly hurt by her mother's assessment of her and yet she didn't know how to dispute it. All her life she had felt weaker, less vital, less interesting than the rest of her family. She had always seemed to be swept along in the bustle of their lives, trying desperately to reach out and touch them and never quite succeeding. She *had* touched people—a few high school and college friends, one or two of her teachers—but with her family, and in particular with her mother, she always seemed to fail. She had never doubted that the failure was her fault. And if she was so unsuccessful with her own mother, how on earth was she going to manage with Ricardo's. She would never admit it to him, but she was really dreading this trip to Colombia.

Chapter Seven

They flew first-class to El Dorado International Airport in Bogotá. Ricardo's sister Elena and her husband were waiting to drive them to the family home in Chico, the elegant new suburb in northern Bogotá. There was a great bustle of kissing and handshaking and Susan had the confused impression of a very attractive woman in her midthirties and a middle-sized, stout man with a gray mustache, before they were all in the car, a deeply cushioned Citroen, and on their way through the darkness. Ricardo sat in the front with his brother-in-law, who had been introduced to Susan as Ernesto Rios, and Susan, holding Ricky, sat in the back with Elena. Up to this point they had all spoken Spanish but now Elena turned to Susan and said, in very good English, "Did you have a pleasant trip? How was the airplane?"

"Very nice," Susan said. Ricky began to fuss and she shifted him to her other shoulder.

"Flying bothers some babies," Elena said sympathetically. "Fortunately, mine always seemed to like it. At any rate, they always slept."

Susan patted Ricky's back and he quieted. "How many children do you have?" she asked.

"Five. But they are no longer little. My youngest is eight." Susan must have looked her surprise for Elena chuckled. "Ricardo is the family baby, did you not know? I am forty and Marta is thirty-eight."

"I knew he had older sisters and nieces and nephews, of course, but that was all."

Ricardo turned around and spoke to his wife in English. "That's the university we're passing, on the right, *querida*." Susan obediently peered out the window but it was too dark to see much.

He smiled. "I'll take you on a tour tomorrow. We can leave Ricky with Mama."

"That would be nice," Susan said faintly.

Ernesto suddenly honked and then rolled down his window to shout something unflattering at the car that had just cut him off.

Ricardo laughed. "Home again," he said. He sounded very content.

The Montoya home in Bogotá was a very large, relatively new Spanish-style house with a walled courtyard on the street that protected it from the gaze of passersby. Ricardo's mother, Maria Montoya, was waiting for them in a beautiful, very formal living room. "Ricardo!" she cried joyfully at the sight of her tall son, and he scooped her up in his arms and hugged her.

When she was on her feet again, he said, "Mama, this is Susan, my wife," and Susan found herself looking at one of the most elegant women she had ever seen in her life. Maria Montoya was a few inches taller than Susan, with graying dark hair worn in a simple chignon and the slim supple figure of a much younger woman. She smiled now at Susan, warmly, and said, "Welcome to Bogotá, Susan."

Susan smiled back. "Thank you, Señora Montoya." She held out her arms. "And here is your grandson."

A look of unutterable tenderness came over the
face of the older woman, and very gently, very competently, she took the baby from Susan. She peered
down into the tiny face and laughed. "*Dios,* Ricardo!
He looks just like you!"

"So everyone says." Ricardo took off his coat, and
Señora Montoya said instantly, "Elena, go and get
Francie."

Elena nodded but, before she went, she took
Ricardo's coat from him. In a minute Elena returned
with a maid who collected the rest of the coats.

"Julio has put your bags in your room," Señora
Montoya said to Susan, "and I have put up Ricardo's
old crib. Would you like to take the baby upstairs?"

"Yes," Susan said gratefully.

"I will show you," her mother-in-law said with a
smile. Then, turning to her daughter, "Elena, see
what your brother would like to eat and drink."

"Yes, Mama," said Elena, and as Susan left she saw
Ricardo sit down on the sofa and stretch out his legs.

When Susan awoke the following morning, she
looked out her bedroom window and saw the mountains. They ringed the city, the peaks of the Cordillera
Central, clear-cut and beautiful against the brilliant
sky. On the plateau was the capital city, Bogotá, with
its curious mix of old Spanish and ultramodern archi-
tecture. But in the future, whenever Susan thought of
Colombia, she would think of the mountains.

She enjoyed her stay in Bogotá very much. She
found Ricardo's mother to be a warm, lovely and
utterly charming woman. At first Susan felt very
young and gauche next to the elegant perfection of
the elder Señora Montoya, but her mother-in-law's
quite genuine kindness soon had her feeling more

comfortable. Both Elena and Marta were very like their mother and Susan spent many pleasant hours chatting with them about babies and child rearing.

Unlike her own mother, the Montoya women were not at all intellectual. They also catered unashamedly to the men of the family—and in particular to Ricardo. For the first time Susan understood why Ricardo expected to be waited on—his mother and his sisters waited on him constantly, hand and foot. He was the only son, and the baby. The whole household, quite literally, revolved around Ricardo. They ate when it was convenient for him. The car was at his disposal; if he was using it, his mother and his wife took taxis. His mother wouldn't dream of making a social engagement without first consulting him. During the whole time they were in Bogotá, Susan never heard Señora Montoya indicate the slightest opposition to a word he uttered.

He was very busy. Half the time Susan did not know where he was or what he was doing. "Business, *querida*," he would answer cheerfully whenever she questioned him as to his doings.

He did find the time to show her around Bogotá, however. They saw all the old Spanish sections of the city, starting with the Plaza de Bolívar. They went to a bullfight at the Plaza de Toros de Santa María, which Susan did not like, and they spent several mornings at the Museo del Oro, Bogotá's Gold Museum. Ricardo was very knowledgeable about the various Indian tribes and their workmanship and Susan found the whole place utterly fascinating.

"I ought to be a tour guide, eh?" he said good-naturedly as they left the museum after their third visit.

"Keep it in mind if you should ever be broke," she retorted, and he laughed.

"I don't think that will ever happen, *querida*. I have my eggs in too many baskets."

One of his baskets was a coffee plantation, a finca, on the mountain slopes three hours out of Bogotá. They went there for a few days the third week of their visit, bringing Ricky with them. Señora Montoya hated to see her grandson removed from her vicinity for so long, but as Ricardo had told his mother humorously, "We can't separate him from his food supply for that long, Mama."

Susan loved the finca. "When I think of Colombia, I shall always think of mountains," she told Ricardo softly as they sat together on the veranda one evening looking at the stars.

"The green mountains of Colombia," Ricardo's voice said next to her in the darkness. "They are the most beautiful in the world."

"And no snow," Susan said incredulously.

"Well, *querida*, we are in the tropics."

Susan laughed. "It's hard to believe that in Bogotá. Your mother has the fire going all the time and I've worn my coat every day."

"That is because Bogotá is at eight thousand feet. In Colombia, if you want a change of climate, all you must do is change your altitude. The finca is warm. Down at sea level, at Santa Marta and Cartagena, it is hot."

It was true. They had driven three hours down the mountains from Bogotá and the weather here was warm and summery. Susan sighed and inhaled deeply. "It's nice just to *sit*," She remarked after a while. "Your mother's energy is astonishing. Every day she has at *least* two social engagements for me to attend.

I'm embarrassed to tell her I'd just like to stay home and do nothing once in a while. Has she always been this busy?"

He laughed and shrugged. "She has her clubs, her luncheons, her teas, just as any woman does." He looked down at her, his face shadowed by the darkness. "You will be just the same, *querida*, once you get a little more established in Stamford."

He reached out with one arm and drew her closer so that she was resting against him, her head falling naturally into the hollow of his shoulder. "I don't know," she said uncertainly. "Somehow, Ricardo, life for me is more—difficult."

"What can be difficult?" he murmured into the baby-fine softness of her hair. "I am here to take care of you now."

It was too hard to explain. But she knew, with great certainty, that she was not the social, urban, clubby person that Ricardo's mother was—or her own mother for that matter. She was the sort of person who needed a few friends, people she could really touch, really talk to and share with. The busyness of a large acquaintance and many social engagements was not for her. And, strangely, she did not think it was for Ricardo either. "*You've* only gone to a few dinner parties," she pointed out after a minute.

She could feel his shoulder move under her cheek in his characteristic shrug. "I don't have much patience for that sort of thing, *querida*."

"No. You've seen the men you want to see during the day, haven't you?"

There was a hint of impatience in his voice. "One can't talk in the crowd of a party."

Susan sighed and closed her eyes. "No. One can't."

His lips moved from her hair down the side of her cheek. "Let's go to bed," he whispered.

And, "All right," she whispered back.

It was raining the day they left the finca. Susan sat in the front of the Fiat Ricardo had borrowed from a friend, holding Ricky in her lap and biting her lip. The road was very steep, narrow, winding and wet and Ricardo was driving much too fast. From time to time she stole a surreptitious glance at his profile. He looked calm, intent, relaxed. He had the car under perfect control. But, he's going too fast, Susan thought again. Ricky moved in her arms. "Ricardo," she said tentatively, "would you mind slowing down a little? You're frightening me."

The car slowed almost instantly. "Of course, *querida*. I'm sorry. I forget you are not used to our mountain roads."

They proceeded up the mountain at a more sedate pace and Susan, glancing again at her husband, felt miserable. He had been enjoying that drive and she had spoiled it. Why was she always so timid, so unadventurous? The only daring thing she had ever done in her life had been that night in the New Hampshire ski lodge when she had made love with Ricardo. She thought about things too much, worried too much. She always had. She supposed she always would. The prospect made her unutterably gloomy. She wished, passionately, that she could be like Ricardo's mother and sisters. None of them would ever have dreamed of asking him to slow down. He really *needn't* have slowed down. He had been in absolute control. But she had been afraid.

She wasn't like his mother or his sisters. She was fond of them. She admired them. But she wasn't like them. They all ran large households, were involved in charitable and church organizations and excelled at a variety of sports. Ricardo's nine nieces and nephews were all healthy, polite, charming children. His sisters were excellent mothers. But it seemed to Susan that the whole life of the Montoya women turned outward. There was nothing left for just themselves.

Perhaps they were right. Perhaps it was through others that one was fulfilled oneself. But she knew also that there was a need in her for something more.

The trip to Bogotá crystallized in Susan the determination to write. For years the journal had been enough: now she must try to use what she had learned and see if she could create something new. It was a need in her that she could not explain, but it was there, as intense as it was inarticulate. Ricardo had said he wouldn't object. She would remind him of that, and when they got home, she would set up a schedule and start to write.

Two days before they left Bogotá there was a very gala party at the San Carlos Palace, home of Colombia's president, which all the Montoyas attended. Señora Montoya took Susan to Bogotá's beautiful shopping center, the Unicentro, and in one of the most elegant and expensive little boutiques she had ever seen Susan got a stunning evening dress. It was dark green with a straight, slim skirt and a bodice that showed off her neck and shoulders gracefully, tastefully but unmistakably. Ricardo loved it and took her out to buy her an emerald necklace and earrings to match. "All good Colombian women wear emeralds," he told her when she protested at the extravagance. "This is your wedding present, *querida*. Wear them in good health."

The emeralds were magnificent and Susan had her hair done in a smooth and sophisticated upswept style in order to better show them off. For the first time she felt as elegant as Ricardo's mother and sisters.

The party was very large and very glittering. All of Bogotá's social elite were there as well as many members of the diplomatic community. At first Susan felt a little overwhelmed by the jewels, the gowns, the darkly handsome men in evening dress. She stayed close to Marta, who introduced her to at least half the people in the room. And then Ricardo came up to her with an elderly, silver-haired man with the aristocratic features of old Spain. "Susan, I would like you to meet Señor Julio Merlano de Diaz," he said. "I know you have read his work."

Julio Merlano de Diaz was Colombia's most famous poet, a winner of the Nobel Prize for Literature. Susan's eyes widened. "I am so pleased to meet you, Señor Merlano," she said in her soft, careful, college Spanish. "I have read almost all of your poems. And I love them. It is a great honor to meet you in person."

Señor Merlano took the hand she had shyly extended and shook it warmly. "Thank you, Señora Montoya. It is my privilege to meet such a charming young lady."

"I reread *The Death of the Condor,* just before we left for Bogotá," she offered a little hesitantly, "and I've been thinking about it ever since. In fact, I've rather been trying to see Colombia through your eyes."

The old man looked at her curiously. "Have you?"

"Yes. It is so—difficult—to have a balanced view, isn't it? To see the dark and the light as well."

Señor Merlano's face was grave. "It is indeed, Señora."

They continued to talk for a few minutes and then

someone came over and collected Ricardo to go and talk to the president. Susan and Julio Merlano moved to a couple of chairs along the wall and continued to talk. *The Death of the Condor* had made a very deep impression on Susan. A long poem about the extinction of a tribe of Colombian Indians, it told of a tragedy that had been perpetrated by a conglomeration of modern political and socially progressive programs. Yet the tone of the poem had not been that of outrage but of sorrow.

"And what have you seen of Colombia through my eyes?" the older man asked at length.

"I've seen a country very like your poem," she replied. She was sitting gracefully on the decorative gilt chair, and in the light of the chandelier her flawless skin glowed with a pearly sheen of indescribable beauty. Her large gray eyes were dark with thought. She tilted her head on its long slender neck and said, "There are things for celebration and things to lament. Ricardo didn't just take me to the tourist sights."

"He didn't, eh?" The famous poet, revered around the world yet regarded with uneasiness in his own country because of his unfortunate penchant for telling the truth, looked across the room at her husband. "Ricardo Montoya is a very extraordinary man," he said softly. "Even more so than his father, I think."

Susan's eyes followed the direction of her companion's. Ricardo was standing on the other side of the room talking to a woman Susan did not know. He was impeccably attired in black-tie evening dress and he looked elegant, assured, cosmopolitan. Yet, even formally dressed and standing perfectly still, he gave the unmistakable impression of strength and agility. As Susan watched he laughed at something the woman had said. His face was instantly transformed by that familiar radiant smile and, watching him, Susan felt something inside her turn over. She stared at her husband, and with that frightening yet unmistakable swerve of her heart all of her feelings of the last weeks crystallized and she knew that she was in love with him.

"I'm sorry," she said faintly to Señor Merlano. "What did you say?"

"I said that Ricardo is a very extraordinary man. I doubt there are five people in this room who have any idea of his activities in Bogotá, and yet all of them regard him as a personal friend."

"Ricardo can be—difficult to know," Susan got out.

"So you understand that," said Señor Merlano, and both of them watched as Ricardo came across the room toward them.

"You have been monopolizing my wife this last hour, Julio," Ricardo said good-naturedly. "What have you been doing?"

"I have been talking to her, Ricardo," the poet replied with gentle dignity. "It is not often I have the chance to converse with so sensitive and intelligent a listener." He smiled at Susan apologetically. "I hope I have not kept you from enjoying the party?"

"Oh no!" Susan was appalled. "It was wonderful talking to you, Señor Merlano. I shall never forget it."

"Nor shall I." The old man smiled at Ricardo. "I only came here tonight to please you, my son. I did not expect to enjoy myself. I must thank you for the gift of your wife's company."

Ricardo smiled back, the warm intimate smile he kept for so few people. "I am leaving on Wednesday, you know. I have left instructions with Ernesto."

"Very good. You won't be returning for a while?"

"No. Spring training starts shortly."

"I see." Señor Merlano looked amused. "You and your baseball."

"I like it," Ricardo returned simply. "It's fun."

"I know." The old man looked even more amused. "You are a constant source of wonder to me, Ricardo." He held out his hand. "Good night, my son."

"Good night, Julio."

The poet turned to Susan. "Good night, Señora Montoya. Ricardo is very fortunate in his wife."

Susan colored with pleasure. "Thank you, Señor."

When the old man had reached the door, Susan glanced up at her husband. She still felt a little dizzy from her discovery of a few minutes ago. She also felt suddenly shy. She looked away from him again and said softly, "He is a splendid person, Ricardo."

"Yes, isn't he? He was a good friend of my father's. I learned quite a lot from him."

"He said . . ." Susan hesitated and then went on. "He said you were doing some special work in Bogotá?"

"It is nothing so special," came the easy answer. "It is merely a matter of helping to fund a few projects." He changed the subject, elusive as ever about his own doings. "You must have bewitched Julio, *querida*. He is usually very quiet."

"He was very kind," she said sincerely. "I was afraid *I* was monopolizing *him*, that he felt he had to stay with me until someone came and took me off his hands."

Ricardo's dark eyes looked down at her and he did not speak for a minute. Then he said, very quietly, "You underestimate yourself, Susan. I have not seen Julio talk so much in a very long time."

"I do love his poems, you see."

"Yes." He smiled again, teasingly. "I see."

Once again Susan felt her heart give that disturbing jolt. She had thought, if she had thought at all, that Ricardo's attraction for her was purely a physical thing. He had a sexual magnetism that was as powerful as it was rare. It was a force felt by nearly every woman who met him. She knew that. She had seen it. She knew also that that was why she had succumbed to him that strange night in New Hampshire.

She had thought that, with effort, they might perhaps build a workable marriage. It had never crossed her mind that she could fall in love with him. He was the total opposite of the kind of man she had thought she could love. They were poles apart in interests, cultural background and temperament. But that moment of revelation at the ball had opened her mind to what her heart had known for quite some while. She loved this dark Latin stranger who had come so disruptively into her life and turned it upside down. She loved him, but she didn't understand him.

It frightened her, this love that had come up on her so unexpectedly. She was afraid of the weakness his presence produced in her. He had only to touch her and she melted; she had no strength to oppose him. He was pleased with her; she knew that. Why shouldn't he be? In all their relationship so far she had conformed to what his idea of a wife ought to be. She had been as docile and tractable as her mother thought her. She had bent before the overpowering force of Ricardo's personality, given in to all his wishes. But if the day came when she had to stand up for herself? If she stopped being what he thought a wife ought to be?

She shivered a little, suddenly cold in the pleasant

heat of the ballroom. He put a warm hand on her bare arm. "Come," he murmured, "let's dance."

"All right," she said, and let him lead her out to the floor. As always, their movement together, to music, enveloped them in a special world. His arms came around her and she rested her head lightly against his shoulder, her eyelids half closing with the sensuous pleasure of his nearness, the feel of his strong body against hers. When the dance ended, she raised her head and found him looking down at her, his eyes dark and unfathomable.

"Susan." It was Marta. "Do come and meet some friends of mine."

"Susan is tired, Marta," said Ricardo pleasantly. "I've just promised to take her home."

"But it's still early!" Marta protested to her sister-in-law.

"Early for you, perhaps," returned Ricardo, "but Susan doesn't like staying up to all hours of the night." Belatedly he turned to her. "Do you, *querida*?"

Her eyes laughed at him although her lips were grave. "No, I'm afraid I don't, Marta," she said. "But it's been a perfectly splendid party."

"I'm glad you enjoyed it," Marta said. "Take the car," she told her brother. "Luis and I will see Mama home."

"Shame on you, Ricardo," Susan said as they got into Señora Montoya's comfortable old Mercedes.

He chuckled and leaned forward to start the ignition. "The things a man must resort to in order to be alone with his wife."

"What if I had wanted to stay?"

"But you didn't," he said serenely.

He was right. She wanted the same thing he did. She watched his profile in silence as they drove through the darkened streets. When they reached his mother's house, he turned to her and said, "It will be good to get home. Then we won't have to find excuses."

She smiled at him, unspeakably pleased by his words. "I thought, perhaps, you regarded Bogotá as home."

He looked surprised and then thoughtful. "I used to," he said at last. "But not anymore." He opened his door and came around the car. "Come," he said. "They'll all be back before we know it." And she laughed.

Chapter Eight

❧

They arrived home in mid-January, after having been in Colombia for over a month. "How was the christening?" Mrs. Morgan asked her daughter when she came to visit a few days later.

"Very lovely," Susan replied. "Ricardo's sister Elena and her husband were godparents, and Ricky wore a christening dress that has been in the family for generations. The archbishop did the job, and I must say it was all very impressive."

"The archbishop?" Mrs. Morgan raised an eyebrow.

"Yes. Ricardo's mother and sisters are very active in church circles. They are really a quite prominent family in Bogotá, Mother."

"I never thought Ricardo was from the barrio," Mrs. Morgan said dryly. "Nor did I think he was so religious."

"Well, actually, he's not," Susan replied a little unwillingly. "Or at least he doesn't go to church much. I think that's another one of those things he leaves to the women."

Mrs. Morgan smiled with real amusement. "I'll tell you, Susan, if Ricardo weren't so outrageously charming, he would be impossible."

"Yes," said Susan slowly, her eyes on her knees. "I know."

"Susan!" The front door banged and the object of their conversation came bursting into the living room, lean and brown and ablaze with life. "Oh, Helen. How nice to see you." And he came across the room to kiss his mother-in-law.

"Was that you I heard sawing wood?" Mrs. Morgan asked. Her face had become very bright and young looking.

"Yes." He grinned, cocky and irresistible. "I'm on my second cord." He shed his vest, which missed the chair and hit the floor. He turned to his wife. "I'm starving, *querida*. What have you got to eat?"

"Would you like some of this banana bread Mother and I have been having?"

"Um. Sounds good. I'll just go wash up first."

He left the room and Susan rose to go to the kitchen. She bent, picked up the vest and then met her mother's eyes. Quite suddenly her face dissolved into laughter. "It's no good telling him to hang it in the closet," she said. "He'll only reply, with irrefutable logic, that it goes upstairs."

When she got back to the living room with the bread, Ricardo had returned. She served him a large slice and a glass of ginger ale and had to refrain from reaching out to smooth back the thick dark brown hair that had fallen over his forehead. He had rolled up the sleeves of his flannel shirt to wash his hands and his forearms looked as hard as iron in the late-winter light.

"Susan has been telling me how much she enjoyed Bogotá," Mrs. Morgan said. "I haven't been there for many years. It sounds as if it's changed."

"It has. There's a lot more money in the city, for one thing."

"Drug money?" Mrs. Morgan asked bluntly.

He shrugged. "Of course, some of it comes from drugs." He took another bite of his bread. "And then in some ways Bogotá hasn't changed at all. There's still the poverty, the street children, the thefts. It will be many years before it approaches the social equality of this country."

Susan sat back and listened quietly to the conversation between her husband and her mother. When Mrs. Morgan got up to leave, Ricardo said, "But why don't you stay for dinner?"

Mrs. Morgan looked immensely gratified. "I'd love to but I can't," she said with regret. "I have a meeting at seven." She turned to her daughter. "I ran into Charlotte Munson the other day, dear. She lives in Stamford, as you know, and she was telling me about the women's club here. They are very active in a wide range of areas and they desperately need more people. And then there's the Junior League. They're starting up a project to work with foster children that sounds very promising."

"I don't think I'd have the time, Mother," Susan hedged.

"Why ever not?" her mother returned impatiently. "Really, Susan, you are so—immovable."

"She has just gotten home from a very long trip," Ricardo said pleasantly. "Give her a chance to catch her breath, Helen."

Her mother's face relaxed. "Yes," she said. "Of course." She kissed Susan and then Ricardo. "Take good care of that grandson of mine."

"I will," promised Susan. "Good-bye, Mother."

"Don't let her push you into doing something you don't want to do," Ricardo said sympathetically as they moved back to the living room.

"You see," Susan explained quickly, "I want to start

to write, and if I fill up my life with other activities, I won't be able to find the time." She smiled ruefully. "Or the energy."

"You must do as you please," Ricardo said again, "not what your mother thinks you should do. You are all grown up now, *querida*."

In the end, however, it was not her mother who put obstacles in the way of her writing but Ricardo. He started out by being very helpful. "Of course you can use the study," he said when she inquired. "I'm starting to do taxes, but that will only last until April."

"Until April?" she echoed incredulously.

"Yes. I prefer to do my own, you see, and it takes time. But I don't work on them every day, Susan. You can use the desk when I don't need it."

"And what about Mrs. Noonan?" Mrs. Noonan was the woman who came in once a week to deal with Ricardo's mail. "Doesn't she always use the study?"

"Yes. But that is only once a week."

"Ricardo, between your taxes and Mrs. Noonan, I'm afraid there isn't going to be much time left for me. I'll find somewhere else to work."

She settled on her old bedroom and Ricardo helped to fix it up, bringing in a larger desk, a typewriter and some bookcases. She was able to get a start on her novel by setting up a schedule that allowed her to work three hours a day in the morning. She actually got the first chapter written.

Then Ricky got sick and she was up with him for two nights in a row.

Then Ricardo came down with the flu. He was used to being splendidly healthy and consequently was a wretched patient on the few occasions when he did become ill. He had a fever and he ached all over and he only wanted Susan. The baby still was not back to sleeping through the night, and after three days of toiling up and down stairs, taking Ricardo's temperature, bringing him medicines and juices and food that he didn't want after he had asked for it, she was exhausted. And frustrated as well. She had actually been *writing*. She had felt the book taking shape for her, the words obeying her thoughts. She wanted to get back to her book. But she hadn't the energy.

Ricardo's fever subsided to a little above normal five days after he first became ill and he seemed more comfortable. That afternoon Susan sat down at her desk and reread her opening chapter. She stared out the window and once more put herself back into the hidden, secret world of childhood. She picked up her pen.

"Susan!" came Ricardo's voice from the next room.

"Yes?" she called back, a hint of impatience in her voice.

"Will you bring me up my account books? They're on the study desk. I think perhaps I could work a little."

Susan sighed, put down her pen, and went downstairs. The books were not on the desk. After two more trips up and down stairs she located them on top of his filing cabinet. She sat down at her desk again, picked up her pen and Ricky woke up. She let him cry for a minute, hoping that Maria would come up to him.

"Susan!" came the voice next door. "I hear the baby."

Susan put down her pen. "Yes, Ricardo," she called with resignation. "I'm going to get him." She did not get back to her book for three more days.

* * *

"We'll be leaving for Florida in a week," Ricardo said to her at dinner a few nights later.

"In a week!" Susan looked at him in astonishment.

"Of course. Spring training begins, *querida*. You know that."

"I didn't know it began so soon. I thought it began in the spring!"

He laughed. "The season begins in the spring, Susan. The training is *for* the spring season. And it has begun in February for years and years."

She put down her fork. "But, Ricardo," she almost wailed, "I've only just gotten home."

"I know." He didn't sound at all sympathetic. "But it is only for six weeks. Then we will be home for the rest of the year."

She picked up her fork again and pushed the rice around on her plate. "I feel like a nomad," she muttered mutinously. "Someone is always pushing me to *go* somewhere."

"Don't be so dramatic," he said coolly, and she looked up to meet his eyes. He was watching her steadily and for once there was no amusement in his face.

"I don't think it's being dramatic to resent being hauled off around the world without even having my wishes consulted," she said. There was bright color in her cheeks. "You gave me four days notice before we went to Colombia. I suppose I should be grateful that you've given me a whole week this time."

"Why do you need notice? Do you want me to give you a schedule for the year?"

At the tone of his voice all the brilliant color drained from her face. "No, I don't want you to give me a schedule," she said a little unsteadily. "I want you to *ask* me. I am your wife, not your slave."

Ricardo's face was closed and shuttered, his eyes cold. "You are my wife and you go where I go," he said evenly. "What is there to ask about? *I* do not have a choice. I must be in Florida on February twentieth." His eyes narrowed. "Or are you saying that you do not wish to come with me?"

"No, I'm not saying that." Susan had been gripping her fork tensely and now she forced herself to relax her hold and set it down. "Of course I want to go with you. But it—upsets—me to have unexpected things flung at me like this. I need time to adjust my thinking."

"So." He took a mouthful of chicken, chewed and swallowed it. "In the future I will try to be less unexpected."

It was not what she wanted but at the moment she knew it was the best she could hope for. She did not want to run the risk of angering him further. She forced a smile. "Thank you, Ricardo."

He shook his head in rueful bewilderment. "Such a tempest in a teapot," he said. "I think I had better make out a schedule after all."

"Perhaps that wouldn't be a bad idea," she said softly.

From upstairs there came the sounds of a baby crying. Ricardo rose. "I'll see to him," he said. Left to herself, Susan collected the plates to bring them out to the kitchen. The crying upstairs stopped and she began to load the dishwasher. Ricardo came downstairs with the baby and sat down with him in a big chair in front of the fire. From the kitchen Susan could hear her husband talking to Ricky in Spanish. When she went into the family room, Ricardo was dancing the baby on his knees and Ricky was beaming. Susan laughed and went over to sit next to Ricardo on the ottoman. They played with the baby for almost an hour and then put him to bed. Susan and Ricardo then followed their son's example, but unlike Ricky, they did not go to sleep for quite some time.

Two days before they left for Florida Ricardo took Susan to the theater in New York. She was aware of the stir his presence caused as they walked through the lobby and could feel herself tightening up, self-conscious and nervous. Ricardo seemed completely at ease, and when a few people said things to him like, "Good luck this season, Rick," or "Are we going to win another series, Rick?" he would smile good-naturedly and make a brief, pleasant response.

"It's a little daunting, being out with such a celebrity," she said to him as they settled into their seats.

He was reading his program. "It's no big deal, *querida*. People in New York just like to wish me well. They are Yankee fans, you see."

The show was a Chekhov revival that had gotten rave reviews. At the intermission Susan turned to her husband and asked curiously, "How are you enjoying it?"

He was looking a little puzzled. "I am enjoying it very much, but it doesn't seem to have a plot. Am I missing something?"

Susan's large gray eyes danced. "Chekhov is short on plot and long on character," she said.

"Oh, I see." The puzzled look left his face and she laughed.

The play was marvelous and the acting superb. At the end, when Sonya was comforting Uncle Vanya with the words: "We must go on living! We shall go on living, Uncle Vanya! We shall live through a long, long chain of days and weary evenings; we shall patiently bear the trials which fate sends us; we shall work for others, both now and in our old age . . ." Susan glanced at Ricardo and saw tears in his eyes.

It was raining when they retrieved their car from the garage and started through the city streets toward the East Side Drive. They were turning down Ninetieth Street when Susan noticed two men on the sidewalk. They were bending over a third man who was lying on the pavement in the rain. "Something's wrong!" Susan said, and Ricardo stopped the car.

"Wait here," he ordered tersely and got out, locking his door behind him. As Susan watched he approached the group. She couldn't hear and so she rolled down her window halfway. They were all speaking Spanish. Then Ricardo knelt on the sidewalk and Susan could see him feeling for a pulse. He spoke sharply to the other two, who Susan could see now were only boys. One immediately ran off up the street like a deer. On the pavement Ricardo began to apply CPR.

Susan reached into the backseat for her umbrella and got out of the car. She went over to stand next to Ricardo and tried as best she could to shelter the man's face with her umbrella. The rain was coming down hard and it was cold.

Ricardo was working very hard. "I don't know CPR, but can I help?" Susan murmured after a minute. He shook his head and kept on counting. The boy knelt next to Ricardo and his young face looked stricken. The second boy came running back. Susan understood him saying that he had called 911 for an ambulance.

It was fifteen minutes before the ambulance arrived and all during that time Ricardo worked ceaselessly over the unconscious man. After the ambulance

workers had taken over, Susan heard Ricardo giving
one of the boys their phone number. The ambulance
pulled away and Susan and Ricardo got back into
their car.

Ricardo started the engine and glanced at her in
concern. "You must be freezing, Susan. I'll get the
heat going as soon as I can."

She was shivering and her feet, clad in thin dress
shoes, were icy. She looked at Ricardo. His hair was
soaked and there was rain still dripping from the tips
of his lashes. His coat looked sodden. He had gotten
the least benefit of the umbrella.

"Do you think he'll be all right?" she asked after
they had driven in silence for a few minutes.

"I doubt it. I couldn't get a pulse going. And I'm not
sure how long he was lying there before we came
along."

"A lot of other cars went by," she said slowly, "but
nobody stopped." He shrugged and said nothing.
"Who were those boys?" she asked.

"His sons. They were all walking home from work.
Evidently he had been complaining of chest pains all
evening."

"Oh dear. It doesn't sound good."

"No, it doesn't."

The heat began to come through and Ricardo
turned the blowers on full blast. They were at the
Larchmont tolls before he said, "What an ending to
our evening out! And I thought I would give you such
a treat tonight."

"It was a treat," she said quickly. "I adored the play.
And the dinner. And I'm very glad we saw that man
when we did. Even if he dies, at least his family will
have the comfort of knowing that everything that could
be done was done. At least they'll know that someone

tried, that they didn't just have to stand helplessly by and watch their father die in front of them."

"I suppose so," he murmured.

"It's true. Why else didn't you give up on him? You said you thought it was hopeless."

After a pause he answered, "As you said, *querida*, one has to try."

She watched the windshield wipers in silence for a few minutes. Then, "I heard you giving one of the boys our phone number."

"Yes. I'm sure they are a poor family. The loss of a father will probably hit them hard."

That was all he said on the subject, but Susan knew he would help the family financially. They pulled into the Greenwich tolls and she turned to look at the suddenly illuminated face of her husband. He was like no one else she had ever known. On the surface he appeared so uncomplicated, so easygoing and casual. But under that surface geniality, he was a very complex man. He could be hard and demanding. He had a temper that frightened her when he was obviously holding it in check. She didn't like to think what he would be like if he were ever really angry. He had enormous magnetism and charm, yet he was a very private man. What he thought and what he felt he kept to himself. Yet he had had tears in his eyes tonight for Uncle Vanya.

He was an enigma to her, a stranger whom she lived with on the most intimate of terms. She loved him—deeply, irrevocably. But aside from liking to sleep with her, she had no idea of how he felt about her. After all, love had not been the reason for their marriage. The rain beat down against the windows of the car and Susan sighed and closed her eyes.

"We'll be home soon, *querida*," he said.

"Yes." The very cadences of his voice did strange things to her insides. He was so splendidly, competently male. Whatever the situation, she could always rest secure in the knowledge that Ricardo would handle it. He had known he might be walking into danger tonight. He had locked her safely into the car before he went to investigate. But he had gone, unhesitatingly. And if there had been danger, she was sure he would have handled that as well. She opened her eyes and looked at his shadowy profile. He was so self-sufficient. He seemed to need no one—certainly not her. The only solid achievement of her life was Ricky. And Ricky was what had brought her Ricardo. He had not even married her for her personal charms.

She closed her eyes again. How was it possible, she wondered, to be so happy and yet so miserable and all at the same time?

Chapter Nine

❧

It was almost impossible to rent a house for only six weeks, so when they went to Florida Ricardo took a large suite in one of the best hotels in Fort Lauderdale. They had two bedrooms, a living room and a small kitchen area with a refrigerator and a hot plate. When they arrived Susan quickly made arrangements for a baby-sitter. "We're going to have to eat dinner out," she told Ricardo firmly, "and I do not want to have to drag Ricky into a hotel dining room every night."

He grinned. "True. His manners leave something to be desired."

"That's putting it mildly," Susan replied. She did not anticipate finding it easy to take care of a four-month-old baby in a hotel suite, but she forebode to press the point. They had had this out before. And difficult though it was probably going to be, she was glad she was here with Ricardo.

She accompanied him the following day when he went to report to the Yankee camp. The sun was shining, it was eighty degrees, and as she pushed Ricky along in his umbrella stroller, she felt the festive mood of the occasion.

They hadn't been at camp for five minutes before Ricardo was surrounded by reporters. He stood courteously, answering their questions with absolute patience and good humor. Susan came in for a small share of the attention but she found the reporters to be polite and their questions had to do with Ricardo and not with her.

"What's Rick been doing all winter?" a wire-service man asked her first.

"Chopping wood," she replied a little shyly. "Building a new garage."

"He looks in great shape."

"Yes. He's been very active."

"Is this the pennant baby?" another reporter asked.

Susan looked startled and then she smiled. "Yes, that's right. He *was* born on the day Ricardo won the pennant, wasn't he?"

The reporter grinned. "It was the *Yankees* who won the pennant, Mrs. Montoya."

Susan laughed. "It all depends on your point of view, I suppose."

The reporter laughed back, his eyes bright with admiration. "I see what you mean. And you're probably not far from the truth. Rick had an awful lot to do with winning that pennant. And the series as well."

She smiled and didn't reply, and shortly afterward Ricardo moved away from the reporters to go change and she and Ricky walked over to where the other wives were sitting to watch. This had been Susan's first encounter with the press and it left her feeling more comfortable than she had dreamed possible. It was the nature of Ricardo's celebrity that protected her, she thought. His personal life was a minor adjunct to his fame. It was what he did on the field that counted.

There had never been a breath in any of the papers about their hasty marriage or the quick arrival of Ricky. The TV announcers had proudly imparted the news of Ricardo's son's birth, but no one had ever mentioned the fact that his parents had only been married for a few months. She had been enormously grateful for their reticence.

And yet Ricardo was one of the most famous men in America. Wherever they went in Florida, people came up to him, for his autograph, to shake his hand, to wish him well. Men and women, teenagers and young boys and girls: the whole world knew Rick Montoya. It knew him—and it admired him. Again and again Susan was struck by the regard in which Ricardo appeared to be held by all the fans who crowded to see him. And she was struck as well by the grace and the courtesy with which he accepted the pressing admiration of so many strangers. Her husband, she thought, was that rarest of all things—a hero deserving of the name.

The change of scene and of routine made it almost impossible for Susan to write. She did try, in the intervals when Ricky was napping, but she had a hard time finding the proper concentration. After an hour's work she would reread what she had written and it would seem terrible: stilted, awkward, childish. When Ricky woke up, she would take him down to the beach and wait for Ricardo to return. He didn't like the idea of her being "cooped up," as he put it, all day in a hotel room. He was such an active, outdoor person himself that he regarded any indoor, sedentary activity as a punishment.

She didn't know why she persisted in her fantasy

that she could write. There was nothing to encourage her to continue; everything seemed to say give it up, be content with what you've got. Yet for her, not to write was not to be fully alive. Writing was the door into her deepest self. And so, though discouraged and feeling foolish, she struggled on.

Florida may not have been good for her writing but it proved to be beneficial in most other ways. Ricardo was happy and that was important to her happiness. And she made a new friend.

His name was Martin Harrison and he was a writer for a very respected literary magazine with a large national circulation. He was not a sports reporter, but he was, as he himself told her, a "baseball nut," and he had come to Florida to do an article on the Yankees for the *National Monthly*. He was in his early thirties, the kind of literate, intelligent, thinking man that Susan had always admired.

She met him about a week after camp opened. She had been sitting in the stands, rocking Ricky with one hand and holding a book with the other, when he came up to her and said in his soft voice, which held just the suspicion of a southern drawl, "Mrs. Montoya?"

Susan looked up from her book and saw a nice-looking man with brown hair and very clear hazel eyes. "Yes?" she said pleasantly.

"I'm Martin Harrison," he explained, "and I'm writing an article about the team for the *National Monthly*. I wonder if I could talk to you for a little?"

"Of course." Susan closed her book and gestured for him to sit down. The warm Florida weather had been good for her this last week. She had been feeling run-down and the sun and the beach had worked wonders. Her skin was tanned to the color of golden honey and her pale hair shone with the texture of spun silk. She was wearing a yellow sun dress and espadrilles and her wide-set gray eyes regarded him with charming gravity. "I'm afraid I'm rather a novice about baseball, Mr. Harrison. Talking to me is likely to prove a dead loss."

"I doubt that," he said, the drawl more pronounced now. Then his eyes lit on her book. "Merlano!" he said. "Do you like him?"

"Yes. In fact," Susan said a little shyly. "I got to meet him last month in Colombia."

They talked for the remainder of the practice session and never once mentioned baseball. In Martin Harrison Susan felt she had met someone from her own world, the world of books and ideas and feelings. When he said, with a rueful laugh, "May I see you again tomorrow? I'm afraid I never got to the point of my interview," she had assented gladly. As she pushed Ricky's stroller across the grass to meet Ricardo she reflected that she had not realized how much she missed the company of people like Martin Harrison. She had let most of her friendships slide this last year—for obvious reasons, she thought wryly. Tonight she would begin to write some long-overdue letters.

She saw Martin Harrison the following day and this time they did talk baseball. They talked about Ricardo as well. "He's amazing, really," Martin Harrison said seriously. "Very few people realize how tough it is to stay at the top of a professional sport. It's got to get to you, that constant pressure to do it again and again. After a while something's got to break—your performance or, in some cases, your willpower. Look at Borg—he just got sick of it all. And who can blame him?"

"Ricardo *likes* to play baseball," Susan said quietly. "He doesn't seem to feel a great deal of pressure."

"But that's why he's so remarkable, don't you see? He's a professional's professional in most ways. He does everything a ballplayer is supposed to do and he does it brilliantly: fielding, throwing, running, bunting. And hitting, of course. But he has the spirit of a kid who plays in the schoolyard for fun. That's why he's so enjoyable to watch, and why he's such a good model for kids. He's so clearly enjoying himself."

Susan looked thoughtfully at the thin, intelligent face of Martin Harrison. "Yes, that's true."

"And he's so—unruffled. No prima donna outbreaks. No temper tantrums. I've never heard him say a mean word about anyone. Since he's been captain, the Yankee clubhouse is a far more pleasant place."

Listening to Martin, Susan felt deeply gratified. It meant something, that a man of this caliber should appreciate Ricardo. When the writer joined her on the beach two days later, she was unfeignedly glad to see him. She was sitting talking to him animatedly when Ricardo arrived from practice. Susan looked up as his shadow fell across her and her small face lit with welcome. "Ricardo!" she said. "Are you out early?"

"No," he said. His dark eyes moved to Martin Harrison and then back to his wife. Susan was wearing an aquamarine maillot suit that showed off her slender figure and pale golden tan. Her loose hair was hooked behind her ears and she wore large dark sunglasses perched on her small, straight nose.

She smiled up at her husband from her sand chair. "We've been talking so much, I lost track of the time."

"Did you, *querida?*" He looked at Martin Harrison, who was sitting cross-legged on the blanket next to a sleeping Ricky. "Have you been discussing baseball?" he asked politely.

Martin laughed and stood up. "No, we've been talking books. Children's books, as a matter of fact. Your wife and I have discovered we shared a common childhood library."

"Oh?" Ricardo looked at Susan. "I'm going to take a swim."

"I'll come with you," Martin said. "It's hot just sitting here." The two men walked side by side down to the water's edge and Susan watched them. Next to Ricardo, she thought, Martin seemed a mere boy, even though he was certainly a few years older. Ricardo dove into the waves and after a brief minute Martin joined him. They swam for quite some time, and when they returned to her they seemed to be in perfect amity. Ricky had woken up and Susan was holding him on her lap when they got back to the blanket. As Ricardo dried his face and hair her eyes briefly scanned him, going over the wide shoulders, flat stomach and narrow hips. He was deeply tanned, his skin dark and coppery, showing, as he once said humorously, his Indian blood. He draped the towel around his neck and she dragged her eyes from his bare torso and looked at Martin Harrison. Next to Ricardo's splendid height and strength he looked pale and insignificant. Ricky began to fuss and Susan rose.

"The prince is hungry," she announced. "I'll go feed him and be back later."

"Why don't you just bring a bottle down to the beach?" Martin asked innocently.

Ricardo's eyes glinted. "Ricky doesn't like bottles," he said. "He likes his mother." The glint became more pronounced. "In that way he resembles his father," he added wickedly.

Susan could feel herself flushing. "Behave yourself," she said primly. "Martin has been telling me what a model of rectitude you are. You don't want him to find out the truth about your character, do you?" And shifting the burden of her son to her other shoulder, she walked toward the hotel as sedately as she could manage in a bathing suit and bare feet. Behind her she could hear Ricardo chuckle.

Martin stayed in Fort Lauderdale for the duration of spring training and Susan found herself seeing quite a lot of him. She didn't think it odd that he should seek out her company. She assumed he felt the way she did—pleased and delighted to have discovered a person who shared so many of the same interests, the same thoughts—and he said nothing to make her think differently. He talked about his writing, and encouraged her to talk about her own.

"You *must* write if that's how you feel," he told her firmly.

"Yes, I know." She smiled a little ruefully. "But it's so hard. Just living seems to take up so much time. And effort. I know now why there were so few women writers in the past. It's very difficult to be married and to write. I've been remembering quite frequently that Jane Austen was single."

"I'm sure Rick doesn't mind your writing," he said carefully.

"Of course he doesn't," she answered quickly. 'I ...
quickly. "It's just that ordinary things seem to take so
much out of me. But that's my fault, not his. Why,
when I look at my mother, I realize what a mountain I
make out of nothing at all. *She* had two children and
managed to find the time to be a working anthropolo-
gist, a college teacher who has published a number of
articles in her field, a wife and an energetic club-
woman. I often just sit back and look at her in amazement."

"You feel things more," Martin said slowly, his eyes
on her delicate, wistful face. He resisted, with diffi-
culty, the desire to reach out and touch her. "You give
one hundred percent of yourself to everything you
do. With you, nothing is part-time. You may not do as
much as your mother, but I'll wager you get a lot more
out of what you *do* do."

"Well," said Susan with an obvious attempt at lightness, "that's a comforting thought. I'll try to hold on to
it." She gave him an apologetic smile. "I'm sorry to be
boring you with my complaints, Martin. It's ridiculous. I have all the modern conveniences, all the help I
want to ask for. I'm just making excuses."

They were together on the beach again and Martin's eyes were drawn irresistibly to the slenderness of
her throat, the high fullness of her breasts. He lay
back on the blanket and shaded his eyes from the sun.
"You don't have the two things every writer needs,"
he said quietly from behind his shielding hand.
"Uninterrupted time and a place to work."

Susan gave a heartfelt sigh. "I'll have it when we get
home," she said. She too moved from a sitting position
to lie on her stomach and prop her chin on her hands.

around these last few months
 e so. I'm a dreadful creature of habit."
 rd on the wing, isn't he?" Martin asked
 essionless voice.
 as to be, I'm afraid." She turned her head and
he uncovered his eyes to look at her. "I'm enough of a
writer to resent sometimes the upheaval of husbands
and babies, but not enough of a writer to do without
them." She smiled a little wryly. "It's the classic feminist dilemma, I fear."

Martin's hazel eyes looked gravely back into hers.
Their faces were very close together. Then he glanced
up. "Rick!" he said. "I didn't see you coming."

Ricardo didn't answer but stood next to the sand
chair looking down at them. Susan smiled at her husband. "Did you win?" she asked. There had been a
preseason game that afternoon.

"No, we lost." He did not smile back but looked
down at her out of half-shut eyes. She sat up and
pushed the hair off of her face.

"What was the score?" asked Martin with an
attempt at casualness. Ricardo's eyes moved, consider-
ingly, to his face.

"Seven–four," he said.

Susan picked up her sunglasses and put them on.
She sensed the tension, Martin thought. "Ricky didn't
wake up in time for me to come by," she said. "Did
anything special happen?"

"No." Ricardo's eyes were very dark and there was a
decidedly grim look at his mouth. Then his gaze
shifted to Martin and the message in that dark stare
was unmistakable.

Martin rose to his feet. "Well, I'll be pushing off.
Good to see you, Rick." He looked at Susan. She was

so very sweet, he thought. So very vulnerable. "Remember what I said," he told her.

She gave him a fleeting smile and then looked again, nervously, at her husband. Martin felt his stomach muscles clench. There was nothing he could do. He managed to return her smile and give a casual wave to Ricardo before he walked away, on rigid legs, down the beach toward the parking lot.

There was silence between Ricardo and Susan after he had left and then Susan started to lie down again. "What did Harrison mean, to remember what he said?" Ricardo asked, and she rose up again and looked at him.

"Oh," she answered uncomfortably, "he just told me to keep on writing. He was trying to be encouraging."

"And I am not encouraging," he said flatly.

"I didn't say that," she protested.

"I see. I'm glad to hear that." He looked at her, measuringly, and then said, "I'm going to swim and then we'll go back to the hotel. It's getting late." He looked at Ricky, who was lying in his basket under the umbrella waving his fists. "Unless you would like to swim first? You must be hot from lying here in the sun."

His courteous offer set her teeth on edge. He was out of temper, and she didn't know why. "No," she replied quietly, "I'm fine. Martin watched him for me before. You go ahead." She watched as he went down to the water's edge and dived in. What could have happened today to put him in such a rotten mood, she wondered. He was making her nervous. She hated it when he was annoyed with her. But she hadn't done anything, she thought in bewilderment. It must have been something that happened during the game. Oh well, she thought with determined optimism, he was hot and he had lost. A swim and dinner should cheer him up.

Chapter Ten

~

They went back to the hotel and Ricardo watched the news while she bathed and fed Ricky. He was still sitting in front of the TV when she came out of the bathroom from her shower and said, with determined cheerfulness, "The bathroom's free if you want a shower." He got up without a word and went inside.

Susan took special pains with her appearance, putting on mascara, which she rarely used, and choosing a hot-pink dress with spaghetti straps and a full skirt. It was a good foil for her tan and her pale hair and Ricardo had said he liked it when she bought it. She clasped a thin gold chain around her throat and was putting on earrings when Ricardo came out of the bathroom. He had a white towel wrapped around his waist and he was scowling.

"I cut myself shaving," he said with great annoyance, and Susan jumped up.

"Oh dear. Let me see it."

"It's all right. But I can't find the alcohol."

"It's in the closet," she said immediately, and went to fetch it for him. He took it from her and went back into the bathroom. He left the door open, and as he raised his hand to apply the cotton swab to his chin Susan saw the muscles in his back ripple. Then there was a knock on the door and she went to let in the girl who baby-sat for Ricky every evening.

They had dinner in the hotel dining room and were joined by Joe Hutchinson and his wife. The extra people relieved the tension between Ricardo and Susan a little and Susan found herself chattering away in a manner quite foreign to her usual quiet self. Ricardo was pleasant although he seemed a little abstracted. They said good night to the Hutchinsons in the lobby and Ricardo said, "Let's go for a walk along the beach. I don't want to go in yet."

"All right," she agreed instantly. "I'm sure Barbara won't mind being out a little late."

It was a beautiful night. The moon hung over the water, huge and silvery, trailing a wake of shimmering light in the dark ocean. Susan took off her high-heeled sandals and Ricardo took off his jacket and loosened his tie. They walked in silence for some time, Susan conscious with every nerve in her body of the man beside her. At first they saw a few other couples but then they came to a stretch of beach that was deserted. Ricardo stopped. Susan halted as well and turned to look at him. Barefoot in the sand, she had to look a very long way up. "Do you want to go back?" she asked.

"Not yet." He spread out his jacket. "Let's sit down."

Without a word she dropped gracefully to the sand. She clasped her arms around her knees and gazed at the moon. "It's so lovely," she said dreamily.

Then he moved, and the sky was blotted out. "So are you, *querida,*" he said, and started to kiss her. She slipped her arms around his neck and when he laid her back onto his jacket, she went willingly, kissing him back, caressing the back of his neck with loving fingers. His lips moved from her mouth to her throat and she looked up at the moon as she felt the warmth of his mouth against her bare skin. The huge silver globe shone serenely down on them and Susan smiled a little. "Diana, the moon goddess, is watching us," she whispered softly. His mouth moved to her breast, and through the thin cotton of her dress her nipple stood up hard. She closed her eyes and slid her fingers into his hair, holding him against her. "Ricardo," she breathed.

"Mmm," he answered, his voice muffled by her body. He slipped a hand under her skirt and began to caress her bare leg. For the first time Susan realized what he intended.

"Ricardo!" she said in a very different tone, and tried to sit up. He moved easily so his body was across hers and, locking his mouth on hers, he stifled her protests. But Susan was horrified. They were lying right out in the open. Anyone could come along. "Ricardo," she hissed when he finally took his mouth away, "stop this. Now. This instant."

"I don't want to." His mouth was moving along the curve of her throat. His hand slid up her leg to her thigh. "Love me," he whispered and kissed her again, softly this time, gently, coaxingly.

"Not here," she muttered against his mouth. But her body was trembling, calling to him.

He pushed her bodice down and his mouth found the fullness of her breasts. His hand moved further up her leg. Her body quivered, reveling in his touch. For a minute she swayed on the edge of surrender. "Susan," he said, his mouth moving against her. "*Amada.*"

"Ricardo," she whispered unevenly, and the word was enough to tell him that he had won. She whim-

pered with pleasure as his weight pressed her back
against the sand, her arms going up to hold him, her
nostrils filled with the scent of him. Her body arched
to the demanding urgency of his and they moved
together in the shattering climax of passion while the
silver moon looked down, silent, beautiful, and indif-
ferent to human desires.

After a long while Ricardo rolled over on his back
and stretched. Slowly, reluctantly, Susan opened her
eyes and came back to reality. She looked at her husband and felt weak with love. "Darling," she said
softly, tentatively. She longed, with every fiber of her
body, to hear him say he loved her.

The moonlight clearly showed her his face. It
looked bright, triumphant. "I knew I could make you
want to," he said. "Little puritan." He laughed.

Susan felt struck to the heart. Was this all he was
going to say to her? She sat up and rested her face on
her knees, her hair swinging forward to hide her face.
"We'd better get dressed," he was saying. "No point in
pushing our luck."

"No," she replied numbly. "I suppose not."

He talked cheerfully as they returned along the
beach, and when she shivered he hung his jacket
around her bare shoulders. His good humor
appeared to be completely restored by her surrender
on the beach. It was Susan, who had surrendered
because she loved him so helplessly, who was left feeling betrayed and forlorn.

They returned to Connecticut at the beginning of
April and on the sixth the Yankees opened the season
at the stadium. Susan went to the game and sat in a
box with a few of the other wives and children. It was
a Sunday afternoon and the huge ball park was

crowded. Out in center field the World Championship banner fluttered in the breeze and the sun was warm on her head.

When Ricardo came to the plate, the whole stadium rose in ovation. He gave his famous, disarming grin, stepped up to the plate and cracked a single into left field. "God, but he makes it look easy." It was Linda Fatato, wife of the Yankee pitcher speaking. "Sal always says one of the best things about being on the Yankees is that he doesn't have to pitch to Rick." Susan smiled in acknowledgment and looked at her husband as he took a lead off first base. There he was, she thought, the most conspicous and most elusive of men. He performed with utter naturalness in front of thousands and yet his deepest self remained a mystery. Susan had no doubt that there were subterranean depths to Ricardo. She had met many people who were all on the surface; what you saw was all there was. Ricardo was not like that. He was like an iceberg—the important part of him remained submerged. She listened to the roar of the crowd as he jogged out to center field and thought that her husband was one of the most solitary persons she had ever known.

With the beginning of the baseball season Susan's life took on a more stable pattern. She had her room back to write in, and Maria was there to take Ricky off her hands for a few hours every morning. She found she was able to write and the book started to take on shape and depth.

She would have been perfectly happy if her relationship with Ricardo had been more secure. As it was, there were times when she felt closer to him than she had ever felt to any other human, when it seemed

they were together in a way she had never found with
anyone else. It happened when they made love, of
course. But it was there at other times as well. The
evenings, for instance, when they would listen to
music, she curled on the end of the sofa and Ricardo
stretched out with his head in her lap. Then the utter
perfection of Bach, so pure and so clear, seemed to be
merely the echo of what there was between her and
this man whom she loved.

But there were the other times as well, the times
when he seemed so far away, so inexplicable, so
beyond the reach of her understanding. His initial tol-
erance of her writing had given way to barely concealed impatience. He did not attempt to infringe on
her time, but she was aware, always, of his irritation,
his disapproval. Consequently she was very careful
not to overrun the time she had set for herself, even
though there were times when she was caught up and
working well and wanted very much to stay for
another hour. But she didn't. She would put down
her pen and physically take herself downstairs even if
her mind was still wrapped up in another world.

One morning, at the end of May, for the first time,
she let herself believe what she knew in her heart of
hearts: she had something publishable. When she
came downstairs to lunch she was still floating in a
cloud. Ricardo had spent the morning mowing the
lawn. He had a night game that evening and was leaving directly after it for a two-week road trip. Susan
smiled at him a little absently and went to get Ricky
from the playpen. She carried him out to the kitchen
and put his jars of food in a baby dish to warm them
up. Ricardo followed her and began to tell her something and she listened for a few minutes without really

hearing him. She had an opening sentence for her next chapter forming in her mind.

"Susan, are you listening to me?" The edge on his voice was what caught her attention.

"I'm sorry, Ricardo." She sounded contrite. "What were you saying?"

"I was telling you that the men are coming to excavate for the pool this week." His face was dark with annoyance. "I won't be here, if you remember, and you must see to it."

"I'm sorry, darling," she repeated. "I was thinking of something else. I'm paying attention now. What do you want me to do?"

He proceeded to give her instructions and she listened carefully, but she could tell from the clipped tone of his voice that he was still irritated. "You've made out a list of your schedule for me, haven't you?" she asked at the end of his lecture. "In case I have to get in touch with you?"

"Susan." He looked even more annoyed. "I have just told you, very clearly, what you must do."

"I know that, Ricardo," she said with gentle dignity, "and I understand what you've said. But I just want to be sure I can get in touch with you. Suppose something happened to Ricky, for instance? You wouldn't want to wait to find out until you called at night, would you?"

"No." He watched as she put a bib on Ricky and propped him up in the high chair. "I've left a schedule and a list of hotels and phone numbers on my desk," he said.

"Good." She spooned some pureed vegetables into Ricky's mouth. "I do wish you didn't have to be away so much," she said as she wiped Ricky's chin with a cloth.

"Do you?" he said. He was standing just behind her and she could feel his eyes on the back of her neck. "Don't forget Miss Garfield will be in on Thursday," he added. "She's the woman I engaged to take Mrs. Noonan's place." Mrs. Noonan, the woman who handled Ricardo's mail, had retired to Florida with her husband.

Susan turned to look up at Ricardo. "Is there anything I need to tell her?"

"Not really. Just make her feel at home. I went over everything with her the other day when she was here."

Ricky yelled and she turned back and fed him another spoonful. Ricardo smiled—she could hear it in his voice—and said, "I'm hungry, too. When is lunch? Where is Maria?"

"Maria's downstairs doing the laundry and lunch will be ready in twenty minutes."

"I'll go shave first." He walked to the kitchen door. "Have you packed for me yet?"

"Not yet. I'll do it after lunch, after Maria puts away the laundry." She turned her head. "Oh, and Ricardo, if you're going upstairs, will you please take your jacket with you?"

"Of course," he replied with absolute courtesy.

Later, when she went upstairs after lunch to pack his suitcase, she saw that he had indeed carried his sweat jacket upstairs. He had also deposited it in a heap on the bed. Susan saw it, frowned and then laughed. "Oh well," she said out loud, "I suppose I mustn't expect miracles. It *was* upstairs. It wasn't on the floor. It'll probably take the rest of my married life to get him to hang it in the closet."

On Thursday the doorbell rang promptly at nine A.M. and Susan called, "I'll get it, Maria!" and went to the door. She had been waiting to greet Miss Garfield and make sure she had everything she needed before disappearing upstairs to her desk. She opened the door and found herself confronting a tall, slim, gorgeous creature who couldn't have been a day over twenty-five. The vision smiled and said, "I'm Vicky Garfield. I've come to work on Rick's correspondence."

"Oh," said Susan blankly. "Yes. Do come in." She held the door open wider and the other girl walked over the threshold. "I'm Susan Montoya," Susan added quickly. "My husband isn't here, but I'll be glad to show you around and help you get started."

"Thank you, Mrs. Montoya." Vicky Garfield smiled. She was at least five feet eight inches tall and she had pitch-black hair and violet eyes. She wore a slim, smart dress and elegant sandals. Next to her Susan felt small, insignificant and frumpy. "Rick explained he would be on the road," Miss Garfield was going on, "and he showed me what he wanted and where to find things when I was here the other day."

That was the second time she had called him Rick. Susan cleared her throat and glanced down at her own dungaree skirt and ancient espadrilles. Her hair needed a wash and she had put it into pigtails for the morning. She felt ridiculous. "Well, then, you know where the study is," she said faintly.

"Yes. Perhaps you could just help me locate this week's correspondence."

"Of course." Susan led the way to the study. Ricardo's desk was in its usual immaculate order. He was as meticulous about his business papers as he was careless about his clothes. "The letters are kept here." Susan pointed to a large wire bin. "Most of them are fan letters from kids, but there are also a lot of requests for appearances, for commercial endorsements and so on. But my husband explained all that to you."

"Yes, he did." The girl smiled politely at Susan. "Thank you, Mrs. Montoya. I suppose I'd better get to work."

Susan smiled back with equal politeness. "If you want anything, coffee or tea or something to eat, Maria will be happy to help you. Have you met Maria?"

"Yes, the other day."

"Oh. Well—good luck, Miss Garfield." Susan closed the study door and went to the stairs, her mind in a whirl. *Where* had Ricardo found that gorgeous creature? And why hadn't his wife been at home when he interviewed her?

She cast her mind back, trying to recall when Ricardo had told her he'd hired a replacement for Mrs. Noonan. It had been about a week ago, she remembered. She had been out for the afternoon, having lunch and going to the new exhibit at the Yale Art Gallery with Maggie Ellis. He'd told her when she got home that he had found someone. She frowned. He'd said she came from an agency. "A modeling agency, most likely," Susan now muttered with unusual waspishness. She did not get very much accomplished on her book that morning.

Miss Garfield finished at two o'clock and sought Susan out before she left. "I've put aside all the mail that needs Rick's personal attention and answered the rest," she said. "Do you want me to stop at the post office and mail it?"

"If you would be so kind," Susan responded formally. "Were there enough stamps?"

"Yes. But we're running low on the pictures that

Rick wanted included in all the answers to his fan mail. Shall I order more?"

"Yes. Yes, I suppose you should."

"All right, then." Miss Garfield gave her a brief, impersonal smile. "I'll see you next week, Mrs. Montoya."

"Yes." Susan's widely set gray eyes did not reflect her own answering smile. "Yes, Miss Garfield, you will."

"Miss Garfield came today," she told Ricardo when he called that night. "She seems very competent. She is going to order some more pictures—she said you were running low."

"Am I? That's the sort of thing Mrs. Noonan always saw to. Evidently Vicky is going to be all right."

He'd called her Vicky. "Yes," said Susan, a little hollowly. "So it seems."

"Have they started work on the pool?" he asked.

"Yes, they came today at last." She filled him in on what had been happening around the house, told him that Ricky was cutting a tooth and listened to his report on tonight's game.

"I miss you," she said softly as he was preparing to hang up.

"I miss you too, *querida*," he said and the dark tones of his voice were like a caress. "I'll miss you even more in a few hours," he added, and now she could hear the familiar amusement. "As a roommate, Joe doesn't compare with a wife."

"Why?" she asked blandly. "Does he snore?"

"I'll explain it to you when I get home." The note of amusement deepened. "In fact, I'll *show* you."

"You do that," she said gently. "Good-bye, darling."

He chuckled. "Good-bye. I'll call you tomorrow."

He hung up and Susan sat quietly for a few minutes staring at the phone. Then she went to pick up Ricky, who was fussing in his playpen. Later, she would watch the game on television. At least that way she would be able to see him. She closed her eyes and rested her cheek against her son's dark silky head. Her stomach muscles were taut and she felt as if someone were squeezing her heart. She loved Ricardo so much. If only she could rest secure in the knowledge that he loved her too.

But he didn't. To love someone meant to share oneself with the beloved, and that Ricardo did not do. She doubted if he ever had with anyone—certainly he did not with his mother or his sisters. But, then, they were only women. Women, in Ricardo's view, had been made for specific purposes—for sex, for motherhood, for ministering to a man's other appetites and needs. In response, men provided women with material comfort and security. That was the view her husband had about marriage—the view he had of her, his wife. She supposed it was a conception that had a lot to recommend it. She could always count on his recognizing his obligations toward her. She knew that he would always, unhesitatingly, put himself between her and any danger the world might threaten her with. If he was autocratic he was also invariably gentle. He had a temper but she had long ceased to fear it. He never allowed it to go beyond mild annoyance and irritation. She wasn't important enough for him to get really mad at her, she thought a little desolately, just as she wasn't important enough for him to confide in. And she couldn't push herself on him. Some things had to be given freely or not at all. She pressed her lips against Ricky's downy head and felt tears sting behind her eyes. Ricky squirmed, seeking her breast, and shakily she laughed. "All right, sweetheart. Mommy will feed you." Blinking hard, she carried the baby into the other room.

Chapter Eleven

Ricardo hadn't been home above a few hours before Susan asked him, "Where did you find Miss Garfield? Didn't you tell me she came through an agency?"

"No, I did not." He gave her a brief, dark look. "You were probably thinking about your book and not listening to me. She's Frank Moyer's daughter."

"You never told me that," Susan said positively.

"I did too." His eyes closed a little and he rested his head against the back of his chaise longue. They were sitting out on the patio in the warm sun. Ricardo had flown into New York early that morning after a night game in California. He had not had much sleep.

Susan looked at his relaxed figure, clad now in running shorts and an old T-shirt. He had the strongest legs of anyone she had ever seen: long, deeply tanned, black-haired and hard as iron. She leaned back in her own chaise and squinted into the sun. "Frank Moyer," she said idly. "Isn't he the man who runs the Y?"

"Yes. I mentioned to him that I was looking for a new secretary and he suggested Vicky. She's in the process of getting a divorce and I guess she's found time hanging on her hands."

"Oh." Susan's eyes swung back to her husband. "Why is she getting a divorce?"

His lashes lifted and his astonishing large brown

eyes regarded her speculatively. "Why all this interest in Vicky Garfield? You aren't jealous of her?"

Susan bit her lip and then, ruefully, she smiled. "Yes, I am. She makes me feel like an untidy little shrimp. The last time she came I even put on makeup and a dress—but it didn't help."

His eyes glinted and a faint smile touched his mouth. "Vicky is getting a divorce because she found out her husband was having an affair with his secretary."

Susan's eyes widened. "He must have been mad," she said. "I mean, *look* at Vicky."

"I have, *querida*," he murmured wickedly, and she frowned. "And what I see," he went serenely on, "is a foolish young woman who runs off to the divorce court at the least sign of trouble." He closed his eyes again. "Women have no sense at all," he said sleepily. Ricardo did not approve of divorce.

"It seems to me Vicky's husband is the one with no sense," Susan said severely. "If he loved her and wanted to keep her, he should have kept his hands off his secretary."

The brown eyes opened again. "Now you are the one who sounds foolish." He held out his hand. "Susan," he said, his voice soft and dark, "let's drop the subject of Vicky. Come here."

She went over to sit on the edge of his chaise longue. "I thought we'd put some steaks on the grill for dinner," she said. "Are you hungry? Do you want a snack first?"

"I'm hungry," he answered. He was holding her hand and now his fingers moved caressingly over the thin skin of her wrist. "But not for food."

"I see," she whispered, and, leaning down, she kissed him, slowly and lingeringly. When she raised her head they were both breathing a little more quickly.

"Let's go upstairs," he said.

"All right," she answered, all thought of Vicky Garfield and her divorce swamped before the rising tide of heat in her blood.

Susan's mother had a party a few days later and both Susan and Ricardo attended. Mrs. Morgan had invited a large crowd of friends, colleagues and neighbors and she had carefully consulted Susan about Ricardo's schedule before she set the day. He had very few days off and Mrs. Morgan was anxious to have her son-in-law present.

Susan had given her mother a date and the party had been scheduled. Ricardo, who knew no one, was soon the center of a large, attentive group and Susan wandered off a little to see if she could do anything to help.

"Susan," said a male voice that sounded oddly familiar. "I've been waiting for you to come."

Slowly Susan turned and looked at the boy—man now, actually, who was facing her under the big maple tree. "Michael . . ." she said wonderingly, "is it really you?"

A familiar wry smile touched his mouth. "It's really me."

"I can't believe it," she said slowly. "It's been so long."

"I know. Too long." His narrow, sensitive face looked much older, she thought. His light blue eyes flashed a look at Ricardo and then came back to her. "I only came because Dad said you would be here. Can we sit down and talk?"

"Of course," she replied instantly. "Let's go to the grape arbor."

She was still there forty minutes later when Ricardo came looking for her. "Ah, there you are, Susan," he said as he came up to her. "I thought you'd gotten lost."

"No." Michael had risen as Ricardo approached and now Susan got up too. "This is Michael Brandon, Ricardo," she said, in introduction. "We grew up together. Michael, my husband, Ricardo Montoya."

Ricardo put out his hand, and after a barely perceptible hesitation, Michael took it. Ricardo said something pleasant and as Michael replied Susan studied the two men before her. Michael only stayed for a few more minutes and ten minutes later Susan saw him leaving the party.

"You're very quiet," Ricardo said to her as they drove home later. "Is it because of that boy you were talking to?"

She sighed. It was a relief to be able to talk about it. "Yes. He's changed a great deal. I must admit he's made me feel very sad."

"You said you grew up together?" His voice sounded detached, impersonal.

"Yes. He was always a year ahead of me in school—from nursery days on up. And we were always good friends."

"Just friends?" he asked.

"No." She stared out the window at the dusk. The trees of the Merritt Parkway were rushing by them. "You're going to get a ticket if you don't slow down," she said automatically, and the car slowed. "He was a brilliant boy," she went on softly, "but he was unhappy. Rebellious. He didn't get on with his father or his stepmother. He was—oh, angry and hurt and he struck out at others because he was so unhappy himself. I understood that, you see. I understood *him*. With me he could be himself." She rested her head against the high seat behind her. "I've always felt I failed him. I cared—but I didn't care enough to give him what he wanted, what he needed."

He grunted and she shot him a quick look. "Not just sex—though there *was* that too. He wanted me to run away and marry him. He'd gone to Harvard, and he was wretched there." She sighed very softly. "He was so brilliant. He made high seven hundreds on both his college board SATs. And then he failed out of college."

"He must have wanted to fail out," Ricardo said noncommittally.

"Yes. I was finishing high school and he wanted us to run away. I didn't want to give up college, give up my own life. What it comes down to is that I didn't love him enough."

"What has he been doing?"

"Oh, Ricardo," the words were a cry of pain, "he's just been drifting around, working on oil rigs, doing odd jobs. He's gotten so—quiet. All the fight seemed to be knocked out of him. Talking to him made me feel like crying."

"It's sad to see a good mind wasted, but you mustn't blame yourself, Susan. A man must find his own way. Either he has the strength to make it, or he does not."

"No," she said after a minute in a very low voice, "that may be true for you, Ricardo, but it isn't true for everybody. I *know* my being with him would have made a difference." She looked out the side window once again. "Poor Michael," she almost whispered.

They finished the rest of the drive in silence.

*   *   *

Ricardo left for another quick road trip the following week, and the day after he had left Martin Harrison called Susan to ask her out to lunch. She was pleased to hear from him and accepted gladly.

It had been quite a while since she had been into New York and she dressed with care and pleasure: a softly woven peach-colored suit and a creamy cotton and linen blouse set off her own coloring quite satisfactorily, she thought. In fact, she felt quite as sophisticated as Vicky Garfield as she stepped into the vestibule of the restaurant Martin had chosen and gave his name to the maître d'.

He was at the table and waiting for her. "Susan." She had forgotten how southern his voice was. "You look marvelous," he said, and sat down again as the waiter seated her.

"Thank you, sir." The gleam of admiration in his hazel eyes was very pleasant. She grinned. "It's fun, coming into New York for lunch. It makes me feel very sophisticated."

"Does it?" The waiter reappeared and Martin asked, "Would you like a drink?"

"Yes." She frowned thoughtfully. "I think I'll have a Bloody Mary." Martin ordered a martini, and as the waiter went away he looked at Susan with smiling eyes.

"Do you want to feel sophisticated?" he asked.

"Well, it's nice for a change. I spend most of the time smelling like milk and baby powder."

"Tell Rick to take you out more," he recommended laconically.

The waiter arrived back with the drinks and set them on the table. Susan raised her glass and said, "Cheers. It's good to see you again."

"It's good to see *you*." He took a swallow of his martini. "I would have called you sooner but I got the distinct impression that Rick was not overly enamored of our friendship."

Susan's eyes widened. "Don't be silly, Martin. Ricardo's not like that."

He smiled a little lopsidedly. "I would be, if you were my wife."

"No, you wouldn't be," she answered serenely. "You'd be happy to know that I had a friend whom I liked very much."

He was studying the olive in his drink. "How is the writing coming along?" he asked abruptly, changing the subject.

"Well . . ." she let out her breath on a long note, and then proceeded to tell him.

"This was just lovely," she said as she finished her coffee an hour and a half later. "I do thank you so much, Martin."

"I meant what I said earlier, you know," he said. "You ought to get Rick to take you out more."

She smiled gently. "Ricardo has a very busy schedule at the moment, I'm afraid. And he really doesn't *like* going out all that much. But we do see people, you know. As a matter of fact, I'm having a party in two weeks—just a backyard picnic. We've built a new pool. I was hoping you'd come."

"I'd love to," he answered immediately. "When is it?"

"June twenty-eighth."

"I'll write it on my calendar," he promised.

"Good."

"Can I get you a taxi?"

"No, thanks. I'm going to do some shopping while I'm here." She gave him a charming, rueful look. "Ricardo has this new secretary who is so elegant that

I feel like a frump every time I look at her. I've decided I need some new clothes."

He looked down at her fair shining head. "You could never look frumpy," he said gravely.

"You haven't seen Vicky Garfield," she retorted. She rose up on tiptoe and kissed his cheek. "Thanks again. We'll see you soon."

"Yes. Soon." He stood in the doorway of the restaurant and watched as she walked away down the street.

Martin duly presented himself at the Montoya residence in Stamford on June twenty-eighth. He parked his car on the wide circular drive behind a lineup of other cars and walked around the house toward the sounds of voices and laughter.

There were about twenty people on the patio and several in the pool. Susan saw him standing there and came across to greet him. "You are looking very fragile and very beautiful in that raspberry dress," he said, and she smiled, not knowing how it lighted up her widely set, luminous eyes.

"I'm so glad you came," she said simply. "There are quite a few people here you must know. Come along and let me introduce you around."

It was a very casual, pleasant party, with food spread on a table in the shade of the patio and a bar where guests could help themselves. Rick came over to greet him and stayed to chat for a while. Martin, who was tall himself, was uncomfortably conscious of the superior height and strength of his host. Ricardo was wearing lightweight khaki slacks and a navy Izod shirt and he looked muscular, lean and very tough. His manner was pleasant but Martin was aware of a cool look in the great dark eyes that made him feel distinctly wary.

There was a little stir among the Yankee players who were standing by the bar and Martin and Ricardo turned to look. A stunningly beautiful girl, tall and slim and raven-haired, was coming out to the patio. "Excuse me," Ricardo murmured to Martin, and went over to greet the new arrival. The girl smiled up at him radiantly and put a hand on his forearm. They spoke together for a few minutes and then Ricardo took her over to the bar to get her a drink and introduce her to the people there. Martin looked for Susan.

He found her deep in conversation with a silver-haired distinguished-looking man and an equally distinguished-looking woman of approximately the same age. As he watched, the woman said something to Susan and she turned toward the bar. The black-haired beauty had accepted a drink from Ricardo and was smiling perfunctorily at the men who were being introduced. That one is only interested in Rick, Martin thought, and he turned back to Susan. She was excusing herself, and as Martin watched she crossed the patio toward her husband. Martin watched in admiration as she greeted the newcomer with gentle dignity. Next to the tall, magnificent, dark-haired splendor of her husband and the other woman she looked very small and slight and fragile. With a sudden flash of insight, Martin realized that this must be the Vicky Garfield who Susan said made her feel like a frump.

A middle-aged Spanish-looking woman came out of the house and crossed to say something to Susan. As Martin watched, Susan excused herself and disappeared inside. Vicky Garfield slid a hand into Ricardo's arm and drew him away toward the pool.

"Mr. Harrison?" a woman's voice said at his elbow.

He turned and found the distinguished woman Susan had been talking to regarding him with a smile. "I'm Helen Morgan," she said, "Susan's mother."

"Mrs. Morgan." He put out his hand to take her extended one. "How nice to meet you."

It was a successful party in that all the guests appeared to have a very good time. Vicky Garfield hung on Ricardo for the whole time, but it was not awkward because Susan did not appear to mind nor did Ricardo appear to take it very seriously. He seemed to be in a relaxed mood, his eyes sparkling with good humor and amused comprehension as he looked down into Vicky's gorgeous face. He did not seem at all smitten, Martin thought. He said something of the sort to Susan.

"I know that," she responded quietly. "She flatters him and he enjoys it. That's all."

He looked at her closely. "After all, in Rick's book, that's what women are for," he said with sudden insight. "Isn't that true?"

Susan was afraid it was all too true, but she wasn't about to say so to Martin. "Not necessarily," she answered coolly. She looked up at him out of remote, gray eyes.

"Where have you gone?" he asked very gently after a moment.

"What do you mean?"

"I mean that you can retreat into yourself faster and put up a No Trespassing sign more successfully than anyone else I've ever known. It can be rather— disconcerting."

Her face relaxed a little. "I'm sorry. I just don't feel like discussing my husband."

"All right, that's fair enough. Now, what about letting me see your book?"

"Oh, Martin." She looked abruptly very young and very vulnerable. "I'm getting cold feet."

"Nonsense. We discussed this at lunch. If it's any good, I'll tell you. And recommend it to my agent. If it isn't any good, I'll tell you that too." He looked at her soberly. "You didn't just write it for yourself, Susan."

She wrinkled her nose. "I know. Well, come along. It's in my study. I've made you a copy."

He grinned. "Good girl," he said, and followed her through the french doors and into the house.

"It went well, I think," Susan said to Ricardo much later, after the last of the guests had driven away.

"Yes, I think so." He smiled a little. "You have the knack of making people feel comfortable, *querida.*"

"Thank you," she said in a low voice.

He yawned and sat down in one of the patio chairs. "I have a sore throat from talking so much."

She sat down herself on a chaise longue and stretched out her legs. "Vicky was such a good audience, I expect you couldn't help yourself."

It was quite dark now and the only light came from the family room through the patio doors. She felt rather than saw him look at her. "She is a beautiful woman," he said. "It's second nature to her to be a good audience for a man." His tone was casual, dismissive.

Susan stared up at the starry sky. No, she thought, Vicky Garfield was not important to him. Which was not to say that he wouldn't sample what she was so clearly offering. After all, he had as much as said he thought marital fidelity was strictly for women. "I shouldn't make the same mistake with Vicky that her husband made with *his* secretary," she said coolly, warningly.

There was a moment of startled silence. Then, "Susan!" He sounded delighted. "You're jealous."

"No, I'm not." There was a pause. "Well, maybe I am," she amended. "You have to admit she's hardly subtle."

"She doesn't intrigue me, *querida*." She saw him move in the darkness and then he was sitting on the edge of her chaise. "You are the one who intrigues me. What were you doing with Harrison for such a long time in the house?"

She was astonished that he had noticed their absence. "I gave him my book to read," she said a little unwillingly. The subject of her book always seemed to cause constraint between them.

"I see."

She looked up, trying to read his face. "I can trust him to tell me if it's any good or not, you see. I—I *need* to know, Ricardo."

"I see," he said again.

She went determinedly on. "If it *is* good, he's going to recommend it to his agent."

There was silence for so long that it became an almost tangible presence between them, then at last he spoke. "I don't make any pretense to possessing Harrison's critical ability, but you never thought to show it to me first?"

She was dumbfounded. "I never thought you would be interested."

He flexed his shoulder muscles almost wearily. "No, I suppose I haven't been very supportive, have I?"

"You've let me have the time to work," she protested. "I *have* appreciated that, Ricardo."

He stood up. "It's late and you must be tired."

"Yes." She let him help her to her feet.

"I rather expected your friend Michael to be here tonight," he said as he locked the french doors.

"I asked him. But he didn't want to come." She sighed. "I don't think seeing me again made him very happy."

"It was not seeing you, *querida*. It was seeing *me* that bothered him."

"Poor Michael," she said.

"Poor Michael, indeed." He took her arm. "Come to bed." She leaned against him gratefully as they went up the stairs together.

Chapter Twelve

A strange man arrived immediately after breakfast the following day and spent the morning closeted in the study with Ricardo. He was a little abstracted over lunch and Susan didn't ask him any questions. She had long since learned that any questions from her would invariably be met by a brief, "It was business," answer. If Martin thought she could hang out a No Trespassing sign, she reflected wryly, he should see Ricardo in action.

The day was pleasantly cool and Ricardo asked her if she'd like to take Ricky and go down to the Stamford Nature Museum. She was delighted by the idea and they packed the baby, the car seat and the stroller into the station wagon for the five-minute drive. Ricky was fascinated by the animals on the small farm and Ricardo and Susan enjoyed them almost as much. After walking about for an hour, they sat down by the lake to watch the ducks and Ricky fell asleep on the grass. "The man who was here this morning was from Latin American Watch," Ricardo said as he slowly threw bread to the birds. "It's a human rights organization that deals solely with Latin America. They've asked me to be on their board of directors."

Susan looked curiously at his expressionless profile. "I see. And what did you say?"

He turned to look at her and the set of his mouth was grim. "I said I'd think about it. I've been involved behind the scene for a few years, but. . . ."

Somehow Susan was not surprised that a human rights organization was one of Ricardo's "business" connections. "But what?" she prompted as his voice trailed off.

"I don't have just myself to consider anymore," he said a little roughly.

"I see," she said, and now she *was* surprised.

"It would involve some trips," he was going on. "And I won't be very popular in some circles."

She hadn't thought of that. Abruptly she remembered the latest headlines from Central America and shivered. He could be in danger. If she knew Ricardo, he would go into this thing wholeheartedly if he went in at all. "You'll probably wind up on everyone's death list," she said faintly.

He laughed but sobered almost immediately. "It won't be as bad as that, Susan. I'm too prominent a figure to be picked off easily. But I want to be honest with you. It will involve me traveling about a bit, and it will probably involve some nasty accusations, too."

She thought again of the unmarked graves and unknown prisons all over the troubled countries of Latin America. The thought of Ricardo lying in one of them made her feel physically sick. "And if I say I don't want you to do it?" she asked uncertainly.

"Don't you?" he responded bluntly.

Nervously she tore at the grass with unsteady fingers. He wanted to do it, she thought. He might do it even if she objected. But he was asking. For the first time, he was asking.

She kept her eyes on her own hands but she felt him there beside her. They were such complete opposites,

she thought. The strong and the weak, the coura-
geous and the fearful, the adventurous and the timid.
Her whole instinct was to keep him safely home by his
own hearth. She clasped her hands around her knees
and cleared her throat. "If you want to do it, then you
should," she said, she hoped firmly.

She could feel some of the tension drain out of him.
"Do you mean that?"

"Yes." She turned to look at him. "I hope you have a
good insurance policy," she added lightly.

He grinned. "It won't come to that, *querida*, I
promise."

"I'll hold you to that," she replied a little tartly. "No
matter how good the policy, you're worth a lot more
to me alive than dead."

His large brown eyes sparkled. "I hope you're not
just referring to financial matters."

She remained grave. "Naturally, I'm referring to
financial matters. What else would I be referring to?"

"I have no idea," he replied, and chuckled at her
look. "I'm not a fish to always rise to your bait."

She made a face at him. "It's getting late and you
have a game tonight."

"That's true." He yawned and stretched and rose to
his feet with easy grace. "You collect the baby and I'll
collect the junk," he said. She had to blink away a sudden tear before she could move to obey his instructions.

Two days after the party Martin called and asked if
he could come up to Connecticut to see Susan. "Of
course," she responded breathlessly.

"I could come up tonight. I have an appointment
this afternoon."

"Tonight will be fine. Oh," she added belatedly, "Ricardo has a night game. He won't be home."

"I know," Martin responded briefly. "I'll see you later, Susan."

Susan did not mention the phone call to Ricardo. She would tell him Martin's verdict later, she thought. The house was quiet, with Maria gone and Ricky asleep, when Martin arrived at about eight o'clock. Susan brought him into the family room and gestured him into a comfortable chair. She herself took the sofa. He was carrying her manuscript and her eyes kept going back to stare at it. "Well?" she said tensely, "What did you think?"

"I thought it was going to be good, Susan," he said deliberately. "Knowing you, I was sure it would be publishable. But I never expected this."

Her gray eyes searched his. "You liked it?"

"I thought it was wonderful. Extraordinary, actually. Where the hell did you learn to write like this?"

Her eyes began to glow. "Oh, Martin, do you mean that?"

"I mean every word of it." He was deadly serious. "You were Kate, of course?"

"Yes." She spoke carefully, hesitantly. "It's not all autobiographical, Martin. The central complication is fiction. But I *did* have an older sister like Jane— beautiful, joyous, intelligent."

"What happened to her?" he asked curiously.

"She died in a car crash two years ago. It was so terribly tragic. Sara was so gifted, so lovely. It just wasn't fair. I suppose in a way this book is my tribute to her."

"But you realize, of course," he said softly, "that the interesting character is the child."

"Kate? Well, of course, she's the filter through which the action is seen. . . ."

"She's the interesting character," he repeated, very definitely. "It doesn't surprise me at all that *she* is the one who grew up to marry the hero."

Susan felt her skin flushing. If only he knew why Ricardo had married her . . . "But you liked it?" she got out.

"I thought it was superb. There are a few rough patches, perhaps, but Susan, I really think it's the best first novel I've ever read."

She glowed with pleasure. "Oh, Martin, it means so much to me to hear you say that! I *thought* it was good, but then I didn't really know." Her small face was alight with happiness. "*Thank* you."

"Thank you for showing it to me." He looked down at the manuscript on his knees. "May I show it to my agent? I'm quite sure he'll be interested."

"Of course you may." She gave a little shiver of excitement. "I'm so *happy*."

He smiled a little crookedly. "Suppose you let me tell you a little about the publishing world," he offered. "You're such an innocent."

Susan might be an innocent, but Ricardo most definitely was not. She would leave all the business arrangements up to him. However, she did not think it would be tactful for her to say as much to Martin and so she smiled and said softly, "That would be very nice, Martin."

They talked about publishing and then about her book again and Susan found herself telling him a little about her own childhood. Before they knew it, it was almost midnight.

"I'd better get going," Martin said as he glanced in deep surprise at his watch. "I had no idea it was this late." He stared at Susan for a minute, his eyes taking in her slender figure clad in a soft, smoky-blue summer dress. "I can never keep track of the time when I'm with you," he said quietly.

Susan smiled at him a little sleepily. "I know. I talk your ear off." Her hair shimmered in the soft light of the lamp and her eyes looked wide and dark and mysterious. "You've been such a good friend to me, Martin," she said.

"I'm afraid friendship is not the emotion I feel for you," he responded a little harshly. "Surely you've sensed that?"

She had been curled up on the end of the sofa and now she sat up and swung her legs to the floor. The corner of her dress stayed caught under her for a minute and he had a brief glimpse of a bare, golden-brown thigh before she pulled it firmly down.

"Susan." He moved to sit beside her on the sofa. "Surely you've guessed by now that I'm in love with you."

Susan stared at him in dumb astonishment. He picked up her hands and bent his head to kiss them. "Please, Martin," she said a little breathlessly. "Don't."

"I tried to stay away from you," he was going on, his voice muffled by her hands. "I didn't call you for months, but then I couldn't stay away any longer. And once I saw you again, I was lost."

"Oh Martin," Susan said in great distress. "I had no idea. And you shouldn't be saying these things to me. I'm not free to listen. You know that."

"You could be," he answered, and still retaining his grasp of her hands, he looked up. "I know it sounds almost ludicrous," he said, "to think that any woman could prefer me to Rick Montoya. But I think I'd be a better husband to you. I understand you, you see." She stared at him out of enormous eyes and slowly, very slowly, she shook her head. "God, Susan," he groaned, "I love you so much." He slid his hands up her bare arms to grasp her shoulders. "Will you at least think about what I've said?"

But Susan wasn't listening. The sixth sense that always told her when Ricardo had entered the room caused her to turn her head and look at the doorway. Her husband was standing there watching them. His face was expressionless but at his side his fists were slowly opening and closing. "Ricardo!" Susan said breathlessly, and Martin dropped his hands from her shoulders.

"Martin was just leaving," she said, and stood up.

"I see," Ricardo answered. He did not sound angry but Susan's eyes were on his clenched fists. Her heart was hammering so hard she thought she would faint.

Martin was very pale. He too got to his feet. "Do you want me to go?" he asked Susan.

She glanced once more at Ricardo before she turned to Martin. "Yes," she said tensely.

Martin hesitated, obviously unsure if he should leave her alone with her ominously silent husband.

Susan was icy with fear but she managed to speak calmly, quietly and with authority. "Martin. Go, please. Now." She stared at him, willing him to obey her, and after another moment's hesitation, he did. Ricardo was still in the doorway and so he went out the french doors to the patio. They could hear the sound of his feet on the stone. Then, a few moments later, came the sound of his car starting up.

Susan hadn't realized she was holding her breath. She let it out now and turned to look at her husband. His hands had relaxed but she saw the little telltale pulse beating in his right temple. "I'm sorry," she said softly. "It was my fault. I should have seen it coming and I didn't."

Still he said nothing and she crossed the room toward him. She was not physically afraid now that Martin had gone. She knew Ricardo would never hurt her. But she had been terrified for Martin. She stopped in front of her husband. "You have a right to be angry," she said humbly. "It was very stupid of me."

"Stupid not to have timed this better?" he said deliberately.

She stared up at him. He had been hurt and now he was trying to hurt back. "Do you think I've been unfaithful to you?" she asked.

He looked down into her clear, truthful eyes. After a minute his face relaxed a fraction. "No, I suppose not," he said. "What was he doing here?"

"He came to bring back my book." All the joy Martin's words had given her were effectively destroyed by this sequel. She had to break through to Ricardo. She couldn't bear the way he was looking at her. "Ricardo," she said, "darling." She put her arms around his waist and laid her cheek against his chest. He was stiff and unyielding under her hands. "We talked about my book," she said, "and then, just as he was leaving, he broke down and said he was in love with me." The look in Martin's eyes came back to her. "He meant it, I think. Poor Martin." She turned her face into Ricardo's shoulder. The scent of him, the feel of him, drove all thought of Martin from her mind. "I'm so sorry," she said, her mouth pressed against his shoulder.

After a very long minute his arms came up to circle her lightly. "He has been in love with you for a long time," he said. "Apparently you were the only one who didn't see it."

The relief she felt at the feel of his arms about her was tremendous. "Did you?" she asked.

"Of course."

She closed her eyes. "Why didn't you warn me?" she murmured.

"I didn't think I had to. I thought all women had a sixth sense for something like that."

It was true, she thought, tightening her arms about his waist. She should have known. But she was so absorbed by Ricardo that she didn't see other men very clearly. "It's bad enough being married to a femme fatale," he was going on, "but an innocent femme fatale is murder."

"A femme fatale? I?" She was so astonished her voice squeaked.

"You." Very, very briefly his cheek came down to touch her hair. Then he released her. "What did Harrison have to say about your book?" he asked.

She longed quite desperately to feel his arms about her once again, but he had put her away from him very definitely. "He liked it," she said.

"I was sure he would." Ricardo sat down in his favorite chair and stretched out his legs.

A thought struck her. "Ricardo, do you suppose he was only saying that because—because of how he feels about me?" she asked in dismay. She dropped down onto an ottoman at his feet.

"No, I don't. What exactly did he say?" She told him, and when she had finished he nodded slowly. "I'm not exactly one of Harrison's admirers," he said then, "but I don't think he'd mislead you on something like this."

"Not deliberately, no. . . ."

"Why don't you let me read it?" he asked.

"I'd love you to read it," she responded instantly. "If you're sure you want to?"

In response he held out his hand. "No time like the present," he said laconically.

She got up from her ottoman and went to retrieve the manila envelope from the sofa. "You don't mean to start reading now?" she asked as she gave it to him. "It's after midnight."

"I'll sleep late tomorrow," he said, and slid the manuscript out of the folder.

She was utterly disconcerted. She had been sure he would want to make love to her tonight, to assert his rights in the face of another claim. And here he was, putting his legs up on her ottoman, making himself comfortable for a long stay. "Well," she said uncertainly, "I guess I'll go up to bed."

"Um." His eyes were on her manuscript. "You'd better. One of us is going to have to get up with Ricky tomorrow."

Very very slowly she trailed off to their room. The whole scene after Martin had left had been very anticlimactic, she thought crossly. Once she had convinced Ricardo of her innocence, he had totally lost interest. And she had been sure he was going to murder Martin! He didn't care, she thought miserably, as she undressed upstairs. So long as she remained sexually faithful to him, he didn't care about her other feelings. She should have let him stew for a while. It would have served him right. She got into bed and curled up under the sheet. She remembered Ricardo's hands, opening and closing so menacingly. No, she thought soberly. On second thought, she had acted in the only possible way. Ricardo had only been a hair's breath from punching Martin. Susan didn't have any illusion as to Martin's chances should such a situation have come to pass. She shivered and burrowed deeper into her pillow. In retrospect, she had gotten off very lightly. And he was even reading her book. She yawned. When you came to think of it, she reflected sleepily, that was really something. She closed her eyes and in two minutes she was asleep.

Ricardo was beside her when she awoke the following morning. She looked for a minute at his dark head on the pillow next to hers and then her eyes traveled down to his strongly muscled shoulders and back. His skin looked very dark and coppery against the white of the sheets. She remembered the feel of that skin against hers, the hard demanding urgency of his body pressing her down into the softness of the bed. Desire ripped through her like a rowel of pain. She closed her eyes, took a deep breath and then slid out of bed. Down the corridor Ricky was crying and she slipped her feet into terry-cloth slippers and went along to her son's room. "Good morning, sweetheart," she said as she opened the door. "Were you calling me?"

Ricardo didn't awake until almost eleven, an unheard of hour for him. He was capable of functioning on far less sleep than she was and was usually up by seven-thirty at the latest. "Good morning," she said brightly as he came down the stairs dressed in old jeans and a light blue knit golf shirt. "You slept well."

He grimaced and rubbed his head. "Too well. Do you have any coffee?"

"Come out to the kitchen and I'll make you some." Maria was on vacation for two weeks and Susan was doing all the chores and the cooking. He followed her out to the shining, modern, white Formica kitchen and sat down at the table. She put coffee in the Farberware instant perk and plugged it in. "Well, don't keep me in suspense," she said. "What did you think of it?"

"I think it is beautiful," he answered simply.

Her heart thudded, skipped a beat and then began to function again. "Do you mean that?" she almost whispered.

"Yes." He looked at her steadily, his brown eyes dark and oddly grave. "I know I'm not a literary type like Harrison, and I read mostly nonfiction these days, but I did take a few Lit courses in college. I know what good writing is. And your book is good. Very good." She smiled at him from across the room, a smile of pure happiness. "It was about Sara, wasn't it?" he asked.

"Yes." She leaned back against the counter. "I wanted to try to capture her, to show what she was like—the warmth, the brightness, the vivid charm of her. It was something I felt I had to do. I wanted to do. For Sara and for Mother."

"And you were Kate," he said quietly.

"Yes." The coffee had stopped perking and she poured him a cup and brought it over to the table. She set out milk and sugar and then poured a cup for herself and came to join him.

"Such a shy, sensitive little girl," he said softly. There was a pause. "And so lonely."

Her head was bent, and she was gazing intently into her coffee. "It isn't easy to be the only weed in the flower garden," she said lightly.

"I think, rather, it was the other way around." He sounded very somber and, startled, she raised her head. "You must publish it," he said, changing the subject.

She hesitated. "Martin said I should get an agent. He offered to recommend me to his." She bit her lip.

"Ricardo, I think I should talk to Martin. He left last night on such an—unpleasant—note. I owe it to him to at least see him and explain." She could feel the heat flushing her cheeks. "I'm dreadfully afraid I led him on," she confessed. "I didn't mean to, but if I'm honest I have to admit he could easily have misinterpreted my actions. I—I do *like* him, you see."

"Yes." His eyes were dark and inscrutable. "I see."

"Then—then you don't mind if I call him?"

"Just this once, Susan." There was a warning note in his voice and she responded hastily.

"Of course. I promise I won't see him alone again."

His long lashes half fell, screening his eyes. "I'm hungry," he said. "I could use some breakfast."

She rose instantly. "What would you like? Eggs? Bacon? Toast?"

"It all sounds good." He watched in silence as she fixed his breakfast, and when it was put in front of him he said, "Thank you, *querida*."

She was standing next to him and bent to drop a light kiss on his thick shining hair. *"De nada,"* she said. Her head cocked. "There's the prince, waking up from his morning nap. I'd better go up to him." Ricardo watched her slight figure move swiftly to the door. It wasn't until she was out of sight that he picked up his fork and began to eat.

Chapter Thirteen

Susan's interview with Martin left her feeling distressed and guilty. She hated to be the cause of someone else's unhappiness and, clearly, she had made Martin very unhappy.

"I shouldn't have spent so much time with you in Florida," she said wretchedly. "I shouldn't have come into the city to have lunch with you. I wouldn't have misled you the way I did if I had been single. All I can say is that I thought my marriage made anything more than friendship between us impossible."

"Not everyone takes marriage so seriously," he had said.

"Well I do."

"And Rick?"

"Ricardo as well. We are married and we plan to stay married, Martin. I'm sorry, but there it is."

She had spoken the truth to Martin, she reflected as she rode home on the early-afternoon train. Ricardo had not married her because he loved her, but he did take his marriage seriously. It was one of the reasons they had been able to make it work. He might not love her, but he respected her position as his wife and the mother of his son. She could not imagine any circumstances under which he would run off to the divorce courts. If he found another woman whom he desired more than her, he would simply make arrangements on the side. Her position would always be secure.

She felt unutterably depressed by the time she got off the train. Ricardo was waiting for her at the station, and as she got into the station wagon next to him she felt like bursting into tears. What did she care about position? It was his love she wanted.

"How did it go?" he asked as they maneuvered through downtown traffic.

"Terrible," she said mournfully. "Poor Martin. I felt so wretched for him. He was really quite serious, I'm afraid."

He grunted. "And what about your book?"

"I'm to call his agent tomorrow. That part at least looks promising."

"Good."

Susan turned around in her seat to smile at Ricky, who was securely belted into his car seat in the back. "How did you make out with the prince?" she asked. It was the first time she had left Ricardo in charge of the baby for more than an hour.

"Very well," he answered peacefully. "I paid bills and answered mail all morning and he zoomed around in that walker you bought him. We managed very well." He shot her a quick, sidelong look. "I even changed his diaper. Twice."

She laughed. "Bravo. Shall I pin on your medal now or later?"

He kept his eyes on the road although a faint answering smile touched his lips. "If you can keep awake until I get home tonight, you can reward me then," he said.

They didn't speak again until they reached home. "I think I'll take a swim before dinner," Susan said as they got out of the car. "The city is like a furnace today and seeing poor Martin has really thrown me. I *hate* to make people unhappy."

"I know you do." Very briefly he touched her cheek. "I think I'll join you. It has been hot today."

They swam for an hour, taking turns swimming Ricky around. The baby loved the water and cried whenever they tried to take him out. "Enough," Ricardo finally said. "I have a game tonight and I won't have the energy for it if I don't sit down for a few minutes." Ricky yelled as his father plunked him down and promptly got his legs up under him to crawl toward the pool again.

Susan snatched him up. "Life has certainly become peppier since Ricky learned to crawl," she said. "We can't leave him here, Ricardo. Get the playpen from the house."

Ricardo wrapped a towel around his waist to keep his bathing trunks from dripping on the carpet and went in through the french doors. He was back in a few minutes carrying the folded-up playpen, which he proceeded to set up in the shade of the umbrella. Susan took off Ricky's wet suit, put a dry Pamper on him and deposited him in the playpen with some of his toys. "Now," she said, "take a nap." Ricky kicked and fussed and both his parents sat down and ignored him. In ten minutes he was asleep.

"I hope he stays as easy to handle as he gets older," Susan said to Ricardo with a smile. "Somehow, though, I doubt it."

"I doubt it too," he answered dryly.

He stretched out on the chaise longue and closed his eyes. Susan regarded his relaxed figure for a minute in silence and then she sighed. "I wish you weren't going away again tomorrow," she said wistfully. He opened his mouth to answer and she said hastily, "I know, I know. It's your job. You tell me that every time. But that doesn't mean I won't miss you."

"Will you, *querida*?" His eyes were still closed.

"Yes, I will."

"That's good." He sounded very sleepy and, annoyed, Susan closed her own eyes.

She must have dozed off, for when she woke Ricardo was gone. After checking on Ricky, who was still sleeping, Susan went into the house. The only sign of her husband downstairs was a wet towel draped over one of the kitchen chairs. She picked it up and went upstairs. Ricardo was in the shower. Susan looked at the clock. It was almost time for dinner. Hastily she pulled off her own suit and put on a pair of navy shorts and a yellow Izod shirt. She tied her hair at the nape of her neck with a yellow ribbon, thrust her feet into sandals and ran back downstairs to put the chicken on the grill and the rice on the stove. When Ricardo came downstairs ten minutes later she was able to say, "Dinner will be in half an hour. I think I heard the paperboy come by a few minutes ago."

He went out to get the paper and sat on the patio reading it as she took Ricky upstairs to change him. When she came back down the rice was done. "I think we'd better eat in the kitchen, Ricardo," she called as she threw a salad together and heated up Ricky's food. "I going to have to feed Ricky as we eat. He's starving."

He came out and took a place at the table. Susan strapped Ricky into his high chair and served up the food. "I'm spoiled rotten," she said as she tried to eat and feed Ricky pureed carrots at the same time. "Maria takes so much off me. I almost forgot to put dinner on."

"I could have gotten something at the ball park," he said. "I didn't want to wake you. You looked tired."

"I was," she admitted. "And depressed, too." She sighed. "Poor Martin."

"Do you know, *querida*," he said, and a curious look of quiet gravity came over his face, "I live in growing dread of one day hearing you say, 'Poor Ricardo.'"

Ricardo didn't go on the road trip after all. A pitch from the Orioles ace relief pitcher connected with Ricardo's head and he ended up in the hospital. Susan, who had been watching the game on TV, was frantic. He had lain still for so long and then she couldn't see him because he was surrounded by trainers and teammates. When the announcer said, "He's moving! He's getting up!" the rush of relief was so overwhelming that she nearly fainted.

Ricardo walked off the field and a runner went to first base for him. Ten minutes later the phone rang. "Susan?" said a male voice. "This is Chuck Henderson." It was one of the team coaches. "Were you watching the game?" he asked.

"Yes," she said tensely.

"Rick seems fine," he said quickly. "Dr. Hastings is going to take him over to the hospital for an X-ray—he most probably has a concussion—but I'm sure he'll be fine. He asked me to call you and tell you that."

"Are they going to keep him overnight, Chuck? He shouldn't drive. Does he want me to come in and get him?"

"They'll keep him overnight." Chuck was positive about that.

"Oh. Will you ask Dr. Hastings to call me after they've checked him over?"

"Sure thing, Susan. Try not to worry. He took a hard crack but the batting helmet absorbed most of the shock. He'll be fine."

"Okay. Thanks for calling, Chuck."

"I'll have Doc Hastings call you later," he promised again. "Try not to worry too much."

"Okay," she said again, and slowly hung up the phone.

The ball game was still on in the family room when she went back inside. "It was a fast ball that got away from Richards," the announcer was saying. "Montoya went down like a shot." Susan switched the TV off and started pacing. She was still on her feet two hours later when the phone rang again. She picked it up on the first ring.

"Hello," she said sharply.

"Mrs. Montoya?"

"Yes. Is this Dr. Hastings?"

"That's right. Rick's going to be fine, Mrs. Montoya, but he has a concussion and the hospital wants to keep him for a day or two."

"I see. How—how serious is the concussion, doctor?"

"He took a good knock. He's got some ringing in his ears and he's dizzy and nauseous. But there doesn't appear to be any serious damage."

Doesn't appear to be. Susan swallowed hard. "When can I see him?"

"You can come in tomorrow if you like."

"Where exactly is the hospital, doctor?" she asked, and wrote down the directions he gave her. It was two when she finally got into bed and nearly five when she finally fell asleep. She was up at seven-thirty and put in a phone call to her mother. Mrs. Morgan was shocked when she heard Ricardo had been hurt and promised to drive down immediately to take care of Ricky so Susan could go to the hospital.

Ricardo looked very white under his tan, and his cheekbones seemed to stand out under his skin. "Oh darling," she said as she went to stand next to the bed. "How do you feel?"

"Lousy," he said frankly. "My head hurts like hell." He moved his head restlessly on the pillow. "Who's staying with Ricky?"

"Mother. She came right down after I called. Can I get you anything?"

"I'm thirsty."

She poured a glass of water for him. His hand was unsteady and she said softly, "Let me hold it." He relinquished the glass to her and sipped it slowly. Then he leaned back and closed his eyes. "The ball got away from Richards, Susan," he said. "He wasn't throwing it at me deliberately."

"Tell that to your aching head," she said a little acidly, and pulled a chair up next to the bed. He smiled faintly. "I'm glad you're here," he murmured. In a few moments he was asleep.

The hospital released him after two more days and he went home for a week. Susan was so glad he was better that she waited on him hand and foot. At the end of the week he went back to the hospital for a checkup and was pronounced fit to play. He immediately made plans to fly up to Boston where the Yankees were starting a four-game series with the Red Sox.

"Can't you at least wait until the team comes home?" Susan protested.

"This is an important series, Susan," he answered. "We were six games up on the Sox when this road trip started and now we're down to three. We can't lose this series."

Susan had not protested any further. What Ricardo had said was true—the Yankees were missing his presence badly. The pennant race had heated up and Ricardo had to play if he was fit. So she packed his suitcase, drove him over to get the limousine to the airport and kissed him good-bye with a smile. She even managed to refrain from telling him to be careful.

The Yankees and the Red Sox split the series in Boston, leaving New York with its three-game advantage, though Ricardo got only one hit in the entire series, a little pop fly that fell just out of the right fielder's reach. He performed brilliantly in the field, however, and the announcers spoke excusingly about his injury so Susan didn't think too much of his unusual lapse.

The slump continued throughout the entire two-week homestand, however, and by then it seemed the whole world had become aware of Ricardo's failure to perform at bat. Newspaper articles were written on the subject. The announcers talked of it constantly. Ricardo's batting average plummeted and the Yankees dropped to two games behind Boston. And always, rarely said outright but constantly implied, was the innuendo that since being hit on the head, Ricardo was afraid of further injury. It was the only reason it seemed anyone could find to account for this most consistent of all players falling into such a catastrophic slump.

It was anguishing for Susan to watch him and yet she had never admired him more than now, when under the most intense pressure from fans, newsmen, coaches, players and most of all himself, he continued to maintain a composure and a courtesy that was nothing short of heroic. He never lost his temper, never allowed an expression or a gesture of anger or despair to escape as he repeatedly struck out or popped out or grounded out and returned quietly to the dugout. To all the myriad questioners he replied simply, "I don't know what's wrong."

Susan didn't know either, but she was utterly certain that fear of injury was not the cause of Ricardo's problem. He received advice from everyone on the team and he tried it all: he changed his stance, he shortened his grip, he moved closer to the plate, he moved further from the plate, but nothing seemed to help.

He did not speak of his slump to Susan as, apart from listening to their suggestions, he did not speak of it to his teammates. Joe Hutchinson called her one day to see if Ricardo was being more open at home than he was in the clubhouse. "Ricardo is a very private man, Joe," Susan said slowly. "He has never been one to talk about his problems or his feelings."

"I know. But, Susan, I really think that's a big part of his present problem. He can't, or he won't get what's bothering him off his chest. I know when I was in a slump last year the only thing that snapped me out of it was talking to people—to my wife, to the other guys—and especially to Rick." He paused. "Can't you try to get him to open up a little?"

"I'll do what I can, Joe," Susan responded quietly. But when she hung up the phone she knew that she was not the one who could open this subject with Ricardo. She trembled to think what must lie behind his apparently unruffled self-command, how the proud and passionate inner man must be feeling in the face of such continual and public failure. She could never be the one to try and breach that self-command. It had to be Ricardo who spoke first. All she could do was be as sensitive as she possibly could to his moods, and to all his other needs.

He never spoke to her of the slump but she sensed in him a need for her company. It was a small consolation, a hidden flower in the wasteland, the fact that in this, the most profoundly distressing time of his career, he did not turn away from her. He didn't want to go out, refused even the simple distraction of a movie that she thought might be good for him. He seemed happiest just sitting quietly with her—around the pool in the afternoon, listening to music at night. Susan thought that he felt comfortable with her because she was a woman and so not one of his peers, his equals.

The team left for another road trip and Ricardo's slump persisted. Susan got to the point of feeling ill every time he came to the plate. How could he stand it, she wondered despairingly. How could he go up there, time and time again, endure the taunts of the fans, the implications of the sports reporters, the doubts he must see in the eyes of his teammates? Where did he find the courage? Where did he find the strength of will?

The team got into New York in the early afternoon and Ricardo was home in time for a swim before dinner. Susan had heard from her agent the day before that he had found a publisher for her book but she had hesitated to tell Ricardo last night on the phone. It did not seem the time to remind him that he had a successful wife. She did tell him over dinner and he seemed to be geniunely pleased, asking her for the details of the contract with a thoroughness she could not begin to answer. "I think you'd better read it when

I get it," she said. "I haven't the foggiest idea of who has what rights. I expect it will all be in the contract. Mr. Wright seemed to think it was a good deal."

"He's supposed to be a good agent," Ricardo admitted. "I checked on him. Still, it's always wise to look things over personally."

After dinner they watched an old movie on TV. Ricardo was very quiet and seemed to be paying attention to the screen, but Susan could sense the tension in him. They went upstairs after the news and Ricardo was in the shower when Ricky woke up and began to cry. He was cutting a tooth and having a very difficult time of it. So was Susan. She gave him some Tylenol and walked him and then rocked him, and finally he fell back to sleep. When she went back into her own bedroom, Ricardo was asleep as well. Susan undressed without putting on the light and slipped quietly into bed so as not to disturb him. She had thought he looked strained and tired and was sure he wasn't sleeping well.

She awoke at three in the morning to find him gone. She got out of bed, and clad only in her thin cotton nightgown, she went downstairs to look for him.

He was sitting in the dark on the patio. He turned his head when he heard the door open and said, "What are you doing out of bed in the middle of the night?"

"Looking for you," she replied, and went to lay her hand lightly on his bare brown shoulder. The muscles under her fingers were rocklike with tension. Susan felt like throwing herself into his arms and weeping, but that was not what he needed. He needed to release some of that terrible tension. She thought she knew what part of the problem was, at any rate. He had been gone for two weeks. Drat Ricky and his tooth, she thought. She put both hands on his shoulders and began to massage them gently. He closed his eyes. "Mmm. That feels good."

She continued with the massage until she felt him relax a little. Then she bent forward so her cheek was against his and her hair swung across his face. "Why don't we go back upstairs?" she murmured. "Ricky is finally alseep."

"Are you trying to seduce me, Susan?" he asked. He sounded grave.

"Yes." She kissed his cheekbone. "I am. If you reject me, I'll be very insulted."

"I would never want to insult you," he said, and stood up. He was wearing only his pajama bottoms as usual and he towered over her in the darkness. She moved closer and put her arms around his waist. He held her very tightly. "I missed you, *querida*," he breathed.

She kissed his chest and then, lightly, delicately, she licked his bare smooth skin. She could feel the shudder that ran all through him and without another word he picked her up and carried her into the house and up the stairs to their bedroom.

She closed her eyes as his weight crushed her into the mattress. His mouth on hers was hard and hungry and his kiss drove her back hard into the pillow. She felt his terrible urgency, his barely controlled desperation. His hands hurt when they gripped her delicate flesh. He groaned and she could sense him making a terrific effort to get himself under control. She opened her eyes. She wasn't ready but it was not her needs that concerned her at the moment. She loved him very very much. "It's all right, darling," she whispered. "You don't have to wait."

His dark eyes looked into hers for a very brief sec-

ond and then he buried his face between her neck and
shoulder. He held her close but his hands now felt
more gentle. After a minute one of them slid down
her shoulder to her breast and began, very lightly to
caress it. Then he turned his head and began to kiss
her throat. Her own hands moved slowly over his
back. "Ricardo," she murmured.

His hand moved down to her stomach and then
moved again. She gasped, pressing up against him.
He locked his mouth on hers and continued to caress
her until she whimpered. His mouth softened and he
said her name, cupping her breasts in both his hands.
She opened her eyes and they stared at each other for
a minute out of passion-narrowed eyes. Then she put
her hands on his hips, pulling him toward her, over
her. She arched up toward him, her breasts filling his hands as she urged him to fill her body, to
complete her, to finish what he had started.

He drove into her and something in her answered
to the hungriness in him, blazing up for him in a bon-
fire of wild sweetness and ecstasy.

"Do you know you always make love in Spanish?"
she asked a long time later. Her head was pillowed on
his shoulder and his hand was sifting gently through
her hair.

"Well, it's my first language, after all," he replied.
"It's the language we almost always spoke at home—
even when we lived in New York."

She sighed with contentment and after a minute his
hand left her hair and moved to her back. Susan's eyes
half closed and she rubbed against him a little, like a
cat being stroked. His hand moved from her back
down to her hip and delicious quivers of anticipation
began to run through her again. "That was like
manna in the desert," he murmured into her ear.

"Shall we do it again?" Very gently his fingers caressed the delicate flesh on the inside of her thigh.

"Mmm," said Susan, moving slightly. "Let's."

Ricardo did not get much sleep on his first night home, but he looked a great deal better as he left for the ball park the following day. Some of the strain at least was gone from his face.

Susan felt better too. It was ineffably sweet to her to know that Ricardo had refused to use her simply to slake his own need. Even though she had given him permission, he had held back and waited for her. He was such a wonderful man, she thought. If only he could break out of this ghastly slump!

Chapter Fourteen

It was Friday night and the Yankees were opening a four-game series with the Red Sox. Boston was four games ahead of them in the pennant race and this series could be crucial. If the Yankees lost, it would be very difficult psychologically as well as statistically for them to ever regain the lead.

Susan's heart was heavy as she turned on the set at eight o'clock to watch. At this point she thought she knew what Ricardo's problem was, but she didn't know how to help him overcome it.

He had lost his confidence. It was as simple as that. He had had a few bad days, which everyone—even Ricardo—had to have once in a while, but because they came right after the accident, people had begun to doubt him. And so instead of simply shrugging and riding out the slump, as she was certain he would have done in any other circumstances, he had tried to prove that he was okay and he had tried too hard. The more he tried, the more tense he became. And the more tense he became, the more impossible it was for him to hit. It was a vicious cycle. The answer was to restore his confidence, but Susan didn't know how to do that. She was the last person he would listen to on the subject of baseball. She had never even watched a game until she had married him.

There was quiet in the stadium as Ricardo came to the plate for the first time. The usual wild cheering his presence had always provoked was replaced this time by a distinctly uneasy silence. There were no boos, no catcalls as there had been on the road. Nor were there any cries of encouragement; just silence. The Yankee fans all seemed to sense the magnitude of what was happening. Ricardo took two strikes and then swung at a bad pitch and grounded it to the first baseman. There was still that eerie silence in the ball park as he returned to the dugout.

He struck out the second time he was up and popped out the third. When the Yankees came to bat in the bottom of the ninth inning, the score was tied at two-two. Joe Hutchinson was the first batter and he singled to center. Rex Hensel, the shortstop, sacrificed him to second. The third batter, Buddy Moran, hit a towering fly to left that was caught at the fence by Boston's Hank Moore. It was two out, the winning run was on second and Ricardo was up. Susan watched him swing his bat and start to move from the on-deck circle toward the plate. Then he paused and looked back at the dugout toward the manager. Frank Henry was coming off the bench and picking a bat out of the rack. Astonishingly, the announcer's voice came over the P.A. "Batting for Montoya, Frank Henry, number nineteen."

A roar went up from the stadium and Susan could hardly see the set through the tears in her eyes and the ache in her throat. This was the final humiliation, being pulled for a pinch hitter in the kind of crisis situation Ricardo had always excelled in. She scarcely heard what the announcers were saying, but the TV camera picked up Ricardo as he sat on the dugout bench. Bert Diaz was beside him, looking upset. Ricardo's face was unreadable.

"That's gone!" the announcer cried loudly, and the camera followed the flight of the ball as it dropped about ten rows back in the right-field stands. The camera then swung to a grinning Frank Henry as he jogged around the bases. His teammates were waiting for him at home plate and the first man to shake his hand was Ricardo.

"Now, there is class," the TV announcer said quietly. "Any other athlete I know would have gone down to the locker room. But not Montoya. I hope to God he can lick this slump. The game can't afford to lose a man of that caliber."

It was after one o'clock when Susan heard Ricardo's car come into the driveway. Ricky had woken up again with his tooth and she was upstairs, rocking his crib, trying to get him back to sleep. Ricardo didn't come upstairs, and when Ricky finally went off some fifteen minutes later, Susan went quietly downstairs. She was wearing a thin summer nightgown and matching peignoir and her bare feet made scarcely any sound on the carpeting.

She found Ricardo in the family room. He was sitting with his elbows on his knees and his knuckles were pressed hard against his forehead. He was rigid with tension. Susan thought her heart would break. "Ricardo," she said out of an aching throat. "Darling, I'm so sorry." She crossed the room to him and he turned in his seat and blindly reached for her. His arms were clamped about her waist, his face pressed against her breasts. "Susan," he groaned. *"Dios,* Susan. I am so scared."

She held him tightly, her lips buried in his hair. "I know, darling, I know," she whispered.

With his face still pressed against her, he began to talk. She had never seen him vulnerable before. She held him close and listened as he poured out his fears, his uncertainties, letting her inside his defenses where no one had ever been before. He held nothing back and in her heart was a strange mixture of pain and aching joy. "Maybe I *am* afraid of getting hurt," he groaned at last in anguish. "I don't know. *Dios*, Susan, I don't know anything anymore!"

She rested her cheek against his smooth dark hair and closed her eyes. She had been right all along, she thought. He was suffering from a catastrophic loss of confidence. Somehow, she had to help him restore it. For the first time he had turned to her and she mustn't fail him now. She took a deep, steadying breath and said calmly, "I know what the problem is, Ricardo."

After a minute his arms loosened and he looked up at her. "You do?" he asked blankly.

"Yes. I haven't said anything because—oh because I was afraid you'd think I was silly."

"*Dios*," he said. "But what is it?"

She looked him directly in the eyes, her own clear and steady and utterly truthful. "You're taking your eye off the ball," she said.

He sat up straight. "What!"

"It's so elementary that I think it needed an amateur like me to pick it up, Ricardo. I thought awhile ago that that might be the problem—simply because I know that was always my problem in tennis when I began to go off my game. And I've watched you for several weeks now. You're so hung up with your

stance and your feet and your swing that you simply
aren't watching the ball."

He stared at her, a look of dawning wonder on his
face. "Can it be?"

"Absolutely. I'll bet you a million dollars that if you
go up to the plate tomorrow, stand any way you like
and simply watch that ball, you'll hit it."

"I'm not watching the ball," he repeated slowly.
"You know, you may be right."

"I know I'm right. It's what's thrown your timing
off. You had a little slump in Boston, which was perfectly natural since you hadn't played for a while, but
then you started fiddling around with your natural
stance. And you got so hung up on fiddling that you
began to take your eye off the ball. So of course the
slump went from bad to worse."

He sat back in the chair and stared over her head,
obviously thinking hard. "I think you're right," he
said after a few minutes of silence. "I think that's
exactly what happened."

"It is," she said positively.

His large brown eyes focused once again on her
face. "You should have told me sooner," he said.

"I would have, but I didn't think you'd listen," she
said hesitantly. "After all, what do I know about baseball?"

"You know something more important in this case,"
he said. "You know me." He shook his head and
laughed. "Taking my eye off the ball. I can't believe
it."

Susan hadn't seen that smile in weeks and her stomach clenched now at the sight of it. Dear God, she
thought, he had actually believed her. She was still
standing in front of him and now he reached up and
pulled her down onto his lap. She put her arms

around his neck and nestled to him. His body felt warm and relaxed against hers. "I'm a genius," she murmured. "It's time you appreciated that."

"I have appreciated you for quite some time now, *querida*," he said softly into her hair.

Susan closed her eyes. Please God, she prayed, let this work. She had no idea if Ricardo were watching the ball or not. She simply thought he needed to feel he would get a hit and then whatever it was that was wrong would correct itself. If this didn't work, he'd never listen to her again. She couldn't bear that, not now when for the first time she was beginning to think that perhaps he did love her after all. He had trusted her tonight. He had let her in. It simply *had* to work.

They stayed like that, peacefully, for a very long time. There was no need to talk, no need to make love even; it was enough that they were quiet and together. Later, upstairs in their bedroom, Ricardo did make love to her with a heartstopping tenderness and passion that drew from her a seemingly bottomless generosity of surrender and of love. She could give to him forever, she felt. There was no one else like him in the world. He fell asleep peacefully in her arms and it was Susan who spent a sleepless night, praying as she had never prayed before, for Ricardo and for their marriage. So much depended upon what happened that afternoon.

Ricardo left for the stadium early to take batting practice. It was Saturday and the Yankees were playing an afternoon game. Susan put Ricky in for his afternoon nap and switched the TV on at two o'clock to watch. She felt sick with apprehension.

Ricardo was the first man to come to bat in the bottom of the second inning. The Red Sox had Paul

Beaulieu, their premier pitcher, on the mound and he had retired the first three Yankees on strikes.

The announcer spoke as Ricardo came up to the plate. "I understand Murphy wasn't going to play Montoya today—he thought perhaps what Rick needed was a break from the pressure. But Rick asked him for one last game." Susan dug her fingernails into her palms. They had been going to bench Ricardo.

The first pitch was a strike. "That was a fastball on the outside corner," the announcer said. "Beaulieu has *very* good stuff today."

There was silence in the ball park as Beaulieu went into his windup. He delivered the pitch and Ricardo swung.

Crack!

Susan knew the sound and watched almost in disbelief as the ball arched into the upper stands. The stadium rose to its feet, screaming hysterically. The Yankee dugout emptied and the whole team was lined up at home plate waiting for Ricardo. "You'd think Montoya'd just won the World Series!" shouted the announcer over the din.

Ricardo's face was serious as he shook the hands of his teammates. It wasn't until Joe Hutchinson slapped him on the back and said something that a smile dawned. At the sight of that familiar grin the noise, impossibly, became even greater. "I think we've got the old Rick back," one announcer said.

"I hope to God you're right," the other responded fervently.

By the time the game was over it appeared the first announcer had been right. Ricardo went three for four and doubled in the winning run in the bottom of the eighth. The slump was over.

Marv Patterson, one of the Yankee announcers,

always had an after-game show when the Yankees played at home and he announced excitedly in the ninth inning that Ricardo was to be his guest. Ricky was crying for his dinner by now and Susan ran out into the kitchen for his high chair, plunked it down in front of the TV and fed him as she watched.

Patterson's introduction was so laudatory it was almost embarrassing and Ricardo's face, as he listened, held the look of faint amusement that was so familiar to Susan that it made her heart turn over. He hadn't looked like that in months. Finally Patterson wound up his panegyric and turned to his guest. "What happened today, Rick?" he asked. "I don't think I've ever seen anyone break out of a slump more dramatically."

Ricardo grinned. "You've probably never seen a more dramatic slump, either."

The announcer laughed. "You're right. It was—awesome."

"It was catastrophic," Ricardo replied cheerfully.

"But what *happened* to cause you to break out of it?"

"My wife solved the problem," Ricardo said. "Last night she told me I wasn't watching the ball."

Marv Patterson stared. "Not watching the ball?" he repeated.

"Yes. It was as simple as that."

"And *your wife* picked it up?"

"That's right." Ricardo looked very serious now. "She's an amazingly observant person, my wife. It comes from being a writer, I guess."

"Is she a writer?" Marv Patterson asked interestedly.

"Yes. Her first novel will be published this spring. It's called *The Flight* and her editor said it was one of the finest first novels he's ever read." Susan stared at her husband in utter astonishment. He was actually bragging about her book!

Marv Patterson was talking to Ricardo now about the pennant race and Susan spooned fruit and vegetables into her son's eager mouth and continued to stare at Ricardo's face on the screen. Never, as long as she lived, would she be able to figure him out.

She was in the kitchen when he came home, and when she heard the door slam she ran out into the hall and flung herself into his arms. "You did it!" she cried joyfully. "I knew you could!"

He swung her off her feet and held her tight. "It was that, more than anything else, that saw me through." He kissed her quick and hard. "The luckiest day of my life was the day a snowstorm blew you to my door," he said, and set her back on her feet.

She laughed unsteadily. "Mine too." She looked up into his face and intoned portentously: "I got the 'man who, more than anyone in our time, has assumed the stature of a hero, an athlete of almost mythic proportions. . . .' "

"Cut it out," he said good-naturedly. "So you watched the postgame show?"

"Of course I did." A terrible din came from the kitchen and Ricardo looked around in alarm. "Ricky's playing in the pot closet," Susan explained, and led the way into the kitchen. Their son was sitting amid a collection of pots and pans and he was banging blissfully. "He's just discovered it," Susan said with a laugh. "It beats all his other toys by a mile in his book."

They didn't get a chance to talk quietly until after dinner and after Ricky's bedtime. Then they went together into the family room and sat on the sofa, Susan in the corner and Ricardo stretched out with his head on her lap. He closed his eyes. "Hmm," he said. "This is nice."

Susan's fingers gently touched his hair. "Mother called today," she murmured after a while. "She invited us to a benefit dance for the hospital. I said I didn't think so but that I'd get back to her. She was annoyed. She said we're worse than hermits, that we never go anywhere."

His eyes stayed closed. He was clearly enjoying the touch of her hand. "We can go if you want to," he said.

Susan sighed. "I suppose we should. It isn't just the slump that's kept us home. We didn't go anywhere before it happened—as Mother pointed out to me."

He opened his eyes. "*Querida*, I'm sorry. I didn't realize that I was turning you into a hermit. Your mother's right. I should take you out more."

Susan smoothed his thick straight hair back from his forehead. "I've never been a social butterfly," she said. "I think it's you Mother is concerned for. You used to go to a lot of parties, or so she informed me."

"I went to parties—and not a lot of them—because I had no one I wanted to stay at home with," he said softly. He reached up for her hand and drew it down to his mouth. "I don't like to go out now because I have to be away so much that when I'm home I don't want to have to share you."

"Oh darling," she whispered. "That's lovely. I'm glad you feel like that." He held her hand against his cheek and she said, cautiously, "Do you know, you sounded almost proud of my book today? You pushed it shamelessly."

He grinned. "I thought I did a very good sales pitch. I got in the title, and when it's coming out." He arched his head back a little so he could see her. "And I *am* proud of it. I'm proud of you."

She looked into his face out of wide, wondering gray eyes. "I always had the impression you didn't like me to write," she said simply.

He relaxed his head once more into her lap. "Yes, well, it had nothing to do with your writing, really," he said a little gruffly.

"But what was it, Ricardo?" she asked curiously.

"It was when you wrote you always seemed so far away from me," he explained awkwardly. "I don't mean physically, but . . ."

His voice trailed off and Susan said, very gently, "Yes, I see."

He laughed a little self-consciously. "I used to think of a poem I studied once in a Lit course in college. It was about a knight who falls in love with an elfin queen and awakens to find himself alone in a cold, empty world."

It took Susan a minute but then she said, "Keats. 'La Belle Dame Sans Merci.'" She quoted softly:

And I awoke, and found me here
    On the cold hill side
And this is why I sojourn here
    Alone and palely loitering,
Though the sedge is withered from the lake,
    And no birds sing.

"Yes," he said, "that's the one." He held her hand tighter. "I know I'm not the kind of man you admire, the kind of man you thought you would marry. I'm not literary or intellectual. But I love you. I can't imagine what life would be without you." He added, a little shakily, "I'd be 'poor Ricardo,' I'm afraid."

"Not the sort of man I admire," she repeated incredulously. "Ricardo, I've never admired anyone more in my life than I've admired you these last months. Can you possibly understand how proud I've been to be your wife, to know that you are the father of my son? But I had no idea how you felt about me. I thought you were just making the best of a difficult situation."

He sat up and swung his legs to the floor. "Are you serious?" he asked in amazement.

"Well . . ." She bit her lip. "Yes." As he continued to stare at her she added defensively, "After all, we hardly knew each other when we married."

"That's true, I suppose." He ran a hand through his hair. "It's hard to remember the time I didn't know you. For so long now I've felt closer to you than to anyone in the world. I never thought I *could* feel like this about anyone. I never used to feel lonely, but now, if I ever lost you. . . ."

His voice stopped and he looked at her. "Oh darling," Susan whispered, and reached up with gentle fingers to smooth the lines from his forehead. "You won't ever lose me. I plan to stick like glue. And even if sometimes my mind is a million miles away, my heart is always, always yours."

"Do you mean that?" he asked gravely.

She reached up and laid her lips gently on his. "I admire you, I love you, I worship you, I adore you," she murmured against his mouth. "What else can I say to convince you?"

"Well." His arms came up to hold her. "You could try showing me."

"I'd love to," she whispered back.

"How about right here?" His eyes sparkled at her with laughter.

She knew he expected her to protest, to insist they go upstairs to the bedroom. "Why not?" she said sweetly, and, sliding her arms around his neck, she pressed the whole length of her body against his.

His reaction was instantaneous and she found herself lying back on the sofa with Ricardo above her. "Kiss me," she whispered. He did and it was long and slow and quite astonishingly erotic. "Do you remember that first time?" she murmured when he moved his mouth down the slender, delicate lines of her throat.

"Mmm," he said huskily. "I'll never forget it."

"I think I knew then what could be between us," she went softly on. "I can remember thinking, I must be crazy, I don't even know this man. But you bewitched me. You always will."

There came the cry of a baby from upstairs and Susan stiffened to listen. "Let him cry for a little," Ricardo said. "At this particular moment, I need you more."

"Ricardo," she said, and let him press her back into the sofa cushions. Her hands went up to hold him close. She had never been happier in her entire life. Ricardo was right; Ricky would simply have to wait.

"THE MOST USEFUL TOOL ANYONE WHO WRITES CAN BUY"

—John Fischer, *Harper's Magazine*

HOW TO GET HAPPILY PUBLISHED
A Complete and Candid Guide
by Judith Applebaum and Nancy Evans
Revised and Updated Edition

All the ways and resources with which to get the very
best deal for your writing and yourself including:

—How to get the words right
—How to submit a manuscript, outline or idea
—How to deal with contracts to get all the money
 you're entitled to
—How to promote your own work
—How to publish your own work yourself
—And much, much more

"EVERYTHING YOU NEED TO KNOW!"—*Boston Globe*

(0452-254752—$6.95 U.S., $8.75 Canada)

Buy them at your local bookstore or use this convenient coupon for ordering.

NEW AMERICAN LIBRARY
P.O. Box 999, Bergenfield, New Jersey 07621

Please send me the PLUME books I have checked above. I am enclosing $_____
(please add $1.00 to this order to cover postage and handling). Send check
or money order—no cash or C.O.D.'s. Prices and numbers are subject to change
without notice.

Name_____

Address_____

City _____ State _____ Zip Code _____
Allow 4-6 weeks for delivery.
This offer is subject to withdrawal without notice.

RAPTURE ROMANCE

Provocative and sensual, passionate and tender— the magic and mystery of love in all its many guises

Coming next month

(0451)

STERLING DECEPTIONS by JoAnn Robb. Entranced by his seductive charm and beguiling blue eyes, Jan Baxter shared a memorable night of glorious passion with Dave Barrie. And though Jan wasn't convinced, Dave called it love—and swore he'd prove it. . .

BLUE RIBBON DAWN by Melinda McKenzie. Billie Weston was swept into aristocrat Nicholas du Vremey's caressing arms and a joyous affair that tantalized her with the promise of love. But Nick's stuffy upper-class circle was far removed from Billy's own. Was the flaming passion they shared enough to overcome the gulf between their worlds?

RELUCTANT SURRENDER by Kathryn Kent. Manager Marcy Jamison was headed straight for the top until Drew Bradford—with his seductive smile and Nordic blue eyes—swept all her management guidelines aside. And though he broke all her rules, he filled her with a very unmanageable desire. She wanted Drew—but was there room in her life for someone who persisted in doing things his own way. . . ?

WRANGLER'S LADY by Deborah Benét. Breanna Michaels wasn't prepared for the challenge of Skye Latimer—who'd never met a bronco he couldn't break, or a woman he couldn't master—for she found herself torn between outraged pride . . . and aroused passion. . . .

TELL US YOUR OPINIONS AND RECEIVE A FREE COPY OF THE RAPTURE NEWSLETTER.

Thank you for filling out our questionnaire. Your response to the following questions will help us to bring you more and better books. In appreciation of your help we will send you a free copy of the Rapture Newsletter.

1. Book Title: _____

   Book # : _____ (5-7)

2. Using the scale below how would you rate this book on the following features? Please write in one rating from 0-10 for each feature in the spaces provided. Ignore bracketed numbers.

(Poor) 0 1 2 3 4 5 6 7 8 9 10 (Excellent)
                                    0-10 Rating

Overall Opinion of Book. . . . . _____ (8)
Plot/Story. . . . . _____ (9)
Setting/Location. . . . . _____ (10)
Writing Style. . . . . _____ (11)
Dialogue. . . . . _____ (12)
Love Scenes. . . . . _____ (13)
Character Development:
Heroine:. . . . . _____ (14)
Hero:. . . . . _____ (15)
Romantic Scene on Front Cover. . . . . _____ (16)
Back Cover Story Outline . . . . _____ (17)
First Page Excerpts. . . . . _____ (18)

3. What is your: Education: Age: _____ (20-22)

      High School ( )1   4 Yrs. College ( )3
      2 Yrs. College ( )2   Post Grad   ( )4 (23)

4. Print Name: _____

   Address: _____

   City: _____ State: _____ Zip: _____

   Phone # ( ) _____ (25)

Thank you for your time and effort. Please send to New American Library, Rapture Romance Research Department, 1633 Broadway, New York, NY 10019.

RAPTURE ROMANCE

**Provocative and sensual,
passionate and tender—
the magic and mystery of love
in all its many guises**

New Titles Available Now—

(0451)

#57 ☐ **WINTER'S PROMISE by Kasey Adams.** A chance meeting brought psychologist Laurel Phillips and a handsome vagabond, Cass, together in a night of unforgettable ecstasy. But, despite their shared love, what future was there for a successful career woman and a rootless wanderer? (128095—$1.95)*

#58 ☐ **BELOVED STRANGER by Joan Wolf.** A winter storm left them in each other's arms, shy Susan Morgan and Ricardo Montoya, baseball's hottest superstar. Even though their worlds were so far apart, Susan found her love had a chance—if she only had the strength to grasp it . . . (128109—$1.95)*

#59 ☐ **BOUNDLESS LOVE by Laurel Chandler.** *"Andrea, your new boss, Quinn Avery, intends to destroy everything you've been working for."* The warning haunted her, even as his sensuous lips covered her with kisses. Was Quinn just using her to further his career? Andrea had to know the truth—even if it broke her heart . . . (128117—$1.95)*

#60 ☐ **STARFIRE by Lisa St. John.** Shane McBride was overwhelmed by Dirk Holland's enigmatic magnetism as he invaded her fantasies—and her willing body. But soon Shane found herself caught in the love-web of a man who wanted to keep *all* his possessions to himself . . . (128125—$1.95)*

*Price is $2.25 in Canada
To order, use the convenient coupon on the last page.

GET SIX RAPTURE ROMANCES EVERY MONTH FOR THE PRICE OF FIVE.

Subscribe to Rapture Romance and every month you'll get six new books for the price of five. That's an $11.70 value for just $9.75. We're so sure you'll love them, we'll give you 10 days to look them over at home. Then you can keep all six and pay for only five, or return the books and owe nothing.

To start you off, we'll send you four books absolutely **FREE.** "Apache Tears," "Love's Gilded Mask," "O'Hara's Woman," and "Love So Fearful." The total value of all four books is $7.80, but they're yours *free* even if you never buy another book.

So order Rapture Romances today. And prepare to meet a different breed of man.

YOUR FIRST 4 BOOKS ARE FREE!
JUST PHONE 1-800-228-1888*

(Or mail the coupon below)
*In Nebraska call 1-800-642-8788

Rapture Romance, P.O. Box 996, Greens Farms, CT 06436

Please send me the 4 Rapture Romances described in this ad FREE and without obligation. Unless you hear from me after I receive them, send me 6 NEW Rapture Romances to preview each month. I understand that you will bill me for only 5 of them at $1.95 each (a total of $9.75) with no shipping, handling or other charges. I always get one book FREE every month. There is no minimum number of books I must buy, and I can cancel at any time. The first 4 FREE books are mine to keep even if I never buy another book.

Name _____ (please print)

Address _____ City _____

State _____ Zip _____ Signature (if under 18, parent or guardian must sign)

 RAPTURE ROMANCE

This offer, limited to one per household and not valid to present subscribers, expires June 30, 1984. Prices subject to change. Specific titles subject to availability. Allow a minimum of 4 weeks for delivery.

RR 183

RAPTURE ROMANCE

Provocative and sensual, passionate and tender— the magic and mystery of love in all its many guises

(0451)

#45	☐	SEPTEMBER SONG by Lisa Moore.	(126301—$1.95)*
#46	☐	A MOUNTAIN MAN by Megan Ashe.	(126319—$1.95)*
#47	☐	THE KNAVE OF HEARTS by Estelle Edwards.	
			(126327—$1.95)*
#48	☐	BEYOND ALL STARS by Linda McKenzie.	
			(126335—$1.95)*
#49	☐	DREAMLOVER by JoAnn Robb.	(126343—$1.95)*
#50	☐	A LOVE SO FRESH by Marilyn Davids.	(126351—$1.95)*
#51	☐	LOVER IN THE WINGS by Francine Shore.	
			(127617—$1.95)*
#52	☐	SILK AND STEEL by Kathryn Kent.	(127625—$1.95)*
#53	☐	ELUSIVE PARADISE by Eleanor Frost.	(127633—$1.95)*
#54	☐	RED SKY AT NIGHT by Ellie Winslow.	(127641—$1.95)*
#55	☐	BITTERSWEET TEMPTATION by Jillian Roth.	
			(127668—$1.95)*
#56	☐	SUN SPARK by Nina Coombs.	(127676—$1.95)*

*Price is $2.50 in Canada.

Buy them at your local

bookstore or use coupon

on next page for ordering.

RAPTURE ROMANCE

*Provocative and sensual,
passionate and tender—
the magic and mystery of love
in all its many guises*

			(0451)
#33	☐	APACHE TEARS by Marianne Clark.	(125525—$1.95)*
#34	☐	AGAINST ALL ODDS by Leslie Morgan.	(125533—$1.95)*
#35	☐	UNTAMED DESIRE by Kasey Adams.	(125541—$1.95)*
#36	☐	LOVE'S GILDED MASK by Francine Shore.	(125568—$1.95)*
#37	☐	O'HARA'S WOMAN by Katherine Ransom.	(125576—$1.95)*
#38	☐	HEART ON TRIAL by Tricia Graves.	(125584—$1.95)*
#39	☐	A DISTANT LIGHT by Ellie Winslow.	(126041—$1.95)*
#40	☐	PASSIONATE ENTERPRISE by Charlotte Wisely.	(126068—$1.95)
#41	☐	TORRENT OF LOVE by Marianna Essex.	(126076—$1.95)
#42	☐	LOVE'S JOURNEY HOME by Bree Thomas.	(126084—$1.95)
#43	☐	AMBER DREAMS by Diana Morgan.	(126092—$1.95)
#44	☐	WINTER FLAME by Deborah Benét.	(126106—$1.95)

*Price is $2.25 in Canada

Buy them at your local bookstore or use this convenient coupon for ordering.

NEW AMERICAN LIBRARY
P.O. Box 999, Bergenfield, New Jersey 07621

Please send me the books I have checked above. I am enclosing $_____
(please add $1.00 to this order to cover postage and handling). Send check
or money order—no cash or C.O.D.'s. Prices and numbers are subject to change
without notice.

Name_____

Address_____

City _____ State _____ Zip Code _____

Allow 4-6 weeks for delivery.
This offer is subject to withdrawal without notice.

RAPTURE ROMANCE

Provocative and sensual, passionate and tender— the magic and mystery of love in all its many guises

(0451)

#19	☐ CHANGE OF HEART by Joan Wolf.	(124421—$1.95)*
#20	☐ EMERALD DREAMS by Diana Morgan.	(124448—$1.95)*
#21	☐ MOONSLIDE by Estelle Edwards.	(124456—$1.95)*
#22	☐ THE GOLDEN MAIDEN by Francine Shore.	
		(124464—$1.95)*
#23	☐ MIDNIGHT EYES by Deborah Benét	(124766—$1.95)*
#24	☐ DANCE OF DESIRE by Elizabeth Allison.	
		(124774—$1.95)*
#25	☐ PAINTED SECRETS by Ellie Winslow.	(124782—$1.95)*
#26	☐ STRANGERS WHO LOVE by Sharon Wagner.	
		(124790—$1.95)*
#27	☐ FROSTFIRE by Jennifer Dale.	(125061—$1.95)*
#28	☐ PRECIOUS POSSESSION by Kathryn Kent.	
		(125088—$1.95)*
#29	☐ STARDUST AND DIAMONDS by JoAnn Robb.	
		(125096—$1.95)*
#30	☐ HEART'S VICTORY by Laurel Chandler.	
		(125118—$1.95)*
#31	☐ A SHARED LOVE by Elisa Stone.	(125126—$1.95)*
#32	☐ FORBIDDEN JOY by Nina Coombs.	(125134—$1.95)*

*Prices $2.25 in Canada

Buy them at your local

bookstore or use coupon

on last page for ordering.

RAPTURE ROMANCE

Provocative and sensual, passionate and tender— the magic and mystery of love in all its many guises

Buy them at your local

bookstore or use coupon

on next page for ordering.

ON SALE NOW!

Signet's daring new line of historical romances . . .

SCARLET RIBBONS

In the decadent world of Shanghai, her innocence and golden beauty aroused men's darkest desires. . . .

DRAGON FLOWER
by Alyssa Welles

Sarina Paige traveled alone to exotic Shanghai not knowing fate was sending her into the storm of rich American Janson Carlyle's lust. But even as his kisses awakened her passion, his demand for her heart without promising his own infuriated her.

Sarina's blonde beauty was a prize many men tried to claim, including the handsome Mandarin, Kwen, who offered her irresistible pleasures on his sumptuous estate and the warmth of his protective love. But Janson offered her the dream of fulfilling her deepest desires, and pursued by these two powerful men, she fought to choose her own destiny. . . .

(0451-128044—$2.95 U.S., $3.50 Canada)

Buy them at your local bookstore or use this convenient coupon for ordering.

NEW AMERICAN LIBRARY

P.O. Box 999, Bergenfield, New Jersey 07621

Please send me the books I have checked above. I am enclosing $_____ (please add $1.00 to this order to cover postage and handling). Send check or money order—no cash or C.O.D.'s. Prices and numbers are subject to change without notice.

Name_____

Address_____

City _____ State _____ Zip Code _____

Allow 4-6 weeks for delivery.

This offer is subject to withdrawal without notice.